"You don't want us to make love?"

Keri was bewildered. Shafe had conspired all day to build the sexual tension to a crackling pitch. Why was he backing away now?

"Odd, isn't it?" Shafe's laugh was a bleak rasp. "I thought I did, but now I can't go through with it. Sex just isn't the answer to everything, or anything. Is it, Keri?"

"I suppose not," Keri replied slowly, wonderingly, not thinking of "sex" but of fond intimacy and ultimate communication between man and wife. "An early night?" she asked, at a loss to know what Shafe was getting at.

"Yes. No. Yes." Shafe uttered an oath. "You're reading me all wrong. We need time to talk our relationship out, and no distractions. No sex."

Keri felt winded. All that had registered was that Shafe did not want her near.

D0424620

ELIZABETH OLDFIELD began writing professionally as a teenager after taking a mail-order writing course, of all things. She later married a mining engineer, gave birth to a daughter and a son and happily put her writing career on hold. Her husband's work took them to Singapore for five years, where Elizabeth found romance novels and became hooked on the genre. Now she's a full-time writer in Scotland and has the best of both worlds—a rich family life and a career that fits the needs of her husband and children.

Books by Elizabeth Oldfield

ELIZABETH OLDFIELD

close proximity

Harlequin Books

TORONTO • NEW YORK • LONDON
AMSTERDAM • PARIS • SYDNEY • HAMBURG
STOCKHOLM • ATHENS • TOKYO • MILAN

Harlequin Presents first edition December 1988
ISBN 0-373-11132-0

Original hardcover edition published in 1987
by Mills & Boon Limited

CHAPTER ONE

PROXIMITY alters *everything*.

Back in London, though her response to Shafe's suggestion had emerged as a masterpiece of restraint—pole-axed by surprise, all she could manage was a faltering affirmative—once the call ended it had erupted into the ecstatic. Snatching up her baby daughter, Keri had whirled laughing around the room. The three of them getting together made marvellous sense, and getting away together on a sun-drenched, palm-studded island even more so. She could hardly wait. Throughout the fortnight during which tickets had been bought, shops scoured for appropriate holiday gear, a pyramid of goods and chattels assembled, she had remained unswervingly buoyant. Angela might make snide remarks, but she had failed to recognise the significance of Shafe taking a full six weeks off work. Even during the long hours flying west across the Atlantic, there had been no qualms. Then, as the stewardess announced their descent into Grantley Adams International Airport, abruptly, and as if in sympathy, Keri's spirits had plunged, her sang-froid had skidded to a halt. A serene and assured woman might have boarded the jumbo jet at Heathrow, but it was a ditherer with nerves wound tight as springs who stepped out into the tropical night.

She hoisted Emma higher up on her hip and pushed the laden trolley forward. Could her optimism have been misplaced? She gave her head a little shake. Impossible. In the sabre-toothed jungle of the media world no one took a month and a half's furlough without having a good reason. A very good reason. And Shafe's reason was that he wanted them to spend time sitting and talking 'like grown-ups'—which meant he had at last wearied of the get up and go routine, and was ready to knuckle down to domesticity. She had always known it would happen some time; the catch had been *when*? Another step ahead and her blue eyes clouded. His adoption of the traditional role of family man was what he intended to discuss, wasn't it? Shouted from a distance of thousands of miles, the answer would have been an emphatic yes! Now, with him standing in the Arrivals hall meagre yards away, nothing seemed certain any more.

'Nearly there,' she muttered, tacking on to the queue which was waiting to pass through Customs.

Something in her tone must have triggered memories of the rehearsals which had interspersed the journey, for Emma jabbed a jubilant and well-sucked finger.

''Lo, Dadda!' she pronounced.

The trilby-hatted object of her greeting swivelled.

'Not me, honeychile,' he said, his grin glittering with gold teeth.

In any other place and at any other time, Keri would have been as amused as the gnarled, coloured gentleman clearly was, but all she could summon up was a half-hearted tweak of the lips. That the fifteen-month-old should accost a total stranger was not so much humorous as an understandable mistake. Indeed, she felt as if she was about to accost a stranger herself, and that it might well turn out to be a mistake, too.

Waved on by a cheery Customs official, she trundled the trolley forwards. From time to time her stomach acted up and now she felt a familiar twinge. She grimaced. Nerves, she supposed. Or could it be abject panic? Keri Rokeby, former slick chick and whiz-bang photographer, was panicking? jeered a voice inside her head. Come *on*! She took a deep breath, switched her emotions into forward gear, and accelerated out through swing doors to face a motley throng of waiting locals, tour company reps and holidaymakers.

Left, right, left, her gaze skittered across the wall of faces. No sign of Shafe. Where was he? He had arranged to fly in from New York yesterday, so he must be around somewhere. Often they had met in similar circumstances—their relationship included a rash of high velocity airport meetings and partings—but his six foot three inches and strong male presence normally ensured instant I-spy. Now the only person behind the barrier who attracted her attention was a broad-shouldered man in a pale pink sports shirt and Levis. Dark gold hair fell in strands across his brow and he had the type of thickly lashed, heavy-lidded grey eyes which guaranteed seduction at fifty paces. The discrepancy was a moustache. For a moment her gaze lingered, flicked off him, then returned.

'Shafe!'

Smiling, he joined her at the exit gap. 'My God, you're astute. Continue the good work, keep your nose clean, and my guess is this time next year you'll be heading the FBI's team of bloodhounds.'

'The moustache confused me,' Keri mumbled, feeling all kinds of a fool.

'Like it? Try it,' he said, and he kissed her. It was a devout, penetrating kiss of considerable panache. Her hard-driving husband never did anything unless it was thoroughly. 'Well?'

His powers of recovery were instant, hers proved sadly otherwise. Instead of her emotions changing up a gear they had gone into reverse, leaving her as weak-kneed and breathless as a teenager on her first date. Add together the two months or more since she had last seen him with the unexpected whiskers on his top lip, and he *did* seem like a stranger—a stranger with a fiendish line in kisses. Hastily Keri struggled to provide a comment. Wholehearted approval would have been the honest reply, yet she hesitated. Given a 'wonderful!' verdict, would he apply it to the look of the moustache, the way it had grazed her skin, or instead to the marauding probe of his tongue? Knowing Shafe's addiction to the sensual, probably the latter.

But was it politic to admit to being bewitched so soon after meeting him again? To let him know nothing had changed; that all he had to do was touch and she became putty in his hands? No, it must be wiser to postpone such declarations until matters between them had been settled. Disposed towards a more conventional life-style he might be, yet his perception of the future could clash with hers, could fall short. Keri's fist tightened on the trolley. The days of being biddable were over. Among her mental baggage lay a set of carefully drafted ground rules; ones he might decline, with thanks. If he did, then she would need to negotiate—negotiate as in 'stick to her guns'. This, in turn, would require whole-hogging fixity of purpose, and thus it made sense to strike an independent note and, temporarily, keep a touch detached.

'Being brushed down at regular intervals'll take some getting used to,' she said flippantly, 'but——'

'You look fantastic,' Shafe cut in.

'Thanks, though after ten hours on a plane I can't say I feel too——'

She dried up. So what if she had hogged the cramped toilet cubicle for a full fifteen minutes while she cleaned her teeth and brushed her hair and softly shaded her eyes? So what if, in a series of contorted gymnastics, she had exchanged crumpled tracksuit for a smart harebell-blue jacket worn over white linen top and slacks? So what if she had chosen high heels when flatties would have been more comfortable? He wasn't speaking to her. In a new gentle voice, he was speaking to Emma.

'Haven't you grown big? Last time I saw you, you were a baby, but now you're a person. And you can walk, so I was informed during one of the ultra-expensive phone calls which your mother and I indulge in.' He held out his arms. 'Say hello to Daddy.'

'Shafe, she's reached the stage where she can be wary, verging on the hostile. All kids go through it. Whenever anyone she doesn't recognise comes along she——'

Her words dried a second time. The toddler, who had screamed blue murder when the woman in the seat across the aisle had dared to pat her silky flaxen curls, had launched herself forward to cuddle close to the father she surely could not remember—or at

least would never identify behind the moustache.
As the proverb said, Keri thought in astonishment,
blood must be thicker than water.

Having taken over their daughter, Shafe took
control of the trolley, wheeling it out across the
concourse to a service road where taxis, buses and
assorted cars were parked.

'Real kind of the airline to allot you one third
of the cargo hold,' he drawled, passing sardonic
eyes over the mountain of luggage. 'Though how
everything'll fit into a mini moke, God only knows.'

'I brought disposable nappies because I was
warned they could be expensive here,' she defended, 'likewise baby lotion and talc. Emma can
be pernickety about food, so the canvas bag con-
tains an assortment of junior meals. You know I
can't go anywhere without the fold-up buggy,
and——' Keri's brows drew together. The aim had
been to present herself as the svelte, cosmopolitan
creature he had first fallen in love with, instead she
was maundering on like the mother next door. If
she was not careful she would find herself regaling
him with theories on potty training. 'I also packed
a few toys,' she finished lamely.

'A few?'

'Say, aren't you Shafe Rokeby of USB News?'
enquired a scrawny middle-aged woman in a
flowered sundress.

'That's correct.'

An arm which rattled with white plastic bangles
semaphored feverishly. 'Phyllis! I was right. It is
him,' she yelled. 'You're the only reason I switch
on television,' the woman informed him as the
hoverer, who resembled an identical twin, ditched
suitcases and scuttled forward to pay eagle-eyed

homage. 'I appreciate a guy who's not afraid of picking up the ball and running, and you run hard. Gee, all those God-forsaken places you report from—Nicaragua, Karachi, downtown Iraq. Even if there are rockets bursting overhead you hang loose. I'm full of admiration. But it's your voice I like best. As I've told Phyllis, it reminds me of bourbon on the rocks: smooth golden brown with just a clink of ice.' She wiggled her hips. 'Sends the most delicious shivers all over me.'

He bowed his head. 'You're very kind, ma'am.'

Emma, not a girl to appreciate someone else receiving attention when *she* was there, thumped Baxter, her beloved fur seal, against his shoulder.

''Lo, Dadda!' she gurgled.

'Is this your little daughter? Didn't realise you were married, but ain't she cute?' Emma reared back from the ringed fingers which attempted to playfully pinch her cheek. 'And this must be your wife?' Keri received a perfunctory once-over. 'I just adore that moustache, Shafe. You wouldn't have any photographs? A signed one would make my day.'

'Sorry, ma'am,' he apologised, with a gracious smile.

His admirer searched in her handbag and produced a dog-eared notepad, plus felt-tip pen.

'Mind giving me a few autographs? Put "To Beryl, fantastic meeting you in Barbados",' she instructed. 'And on the next page, "Happy viewing, Nancy, from Shafe". I also need one for Marilu, she'd never forgive me if I left her out. Write something mushy to her.'

As orders were given and he obliged, Keri watched on in wry amusement. That a man who, at times, could demonstrate a pitifully low private tolerance level should possess such a highly developed public one never ceased to amaze. He was not recognised too often, thanks to determinedly 'keeping his head below the parapet' as he put it, but whenever it happened the fast-moving television reporter Shafe Rokeby accommodatingly braked and became patience personified.

'You're wasted covering trouble spots. Tell the network to give you a programme of your own. You'd make a fabulous game-show host,' his fan informed him, blind to how a dark gold brow quirked. 'Remember that special extra-long interview you did from Paris about a month ago? Terrorists had held those folks at gunpoint in an art gallery, and after they were released you spoke to a minister in charge of——'

'If we don't check in now we could miss our flight,' Phyllis interrupted apologetically, as an announcement over the public address system caught her attention.

Her companion sighed and packed the notepad away. 'It's been real nice meetin' ya, Shafe. And you, little girl.' There was another attempted pinch, another lurching back. 'And you, Mrs Rokeby,' she tossed in as she turned. ''Bye for now.'

''Bye for ever, please be,' Keri muttered, as the women hurried away.

He grinned, resuming their trek towards a battered yellow moke. 'Tsk, tsk. They're the ones who keep me in work, and who will hopefully allow this——' he bussed Emma's cheek and made her giggle '——gorgeous girl to be educated at the best schools, wear the finest clothes, consume nothing but oysters and caviar.'

'I wasn't aware you'd been in Paris,' Keri remarked, taking possession of the toddler again as Shafe stopped the trolley and set about stacking the luggage inside the vehicle. 'Why did the network use you and not the man who's based there?'

'He'd gone off on a fact-finding mission to deepest darkest Chad or some place, so I volunteered to take over. I was able to get to France quicker than him.'

She darted a glance from beneath lowered lashes. 'Did you fly direct from New York?'

Shafe jammed the canvas bag in beside a baby chair which had been fixed on to the rear seat. 'Nope, I stopped off in London to see you. Once on my way there at the beginning of the week, and again on my way back towards the end.' His voice had grown heavy on ice, weak on bourbon. 'Your father's house was locked and empty. A neighbour informed me that both you and your sister had gone off on holiday. Angela had decided to fricassee herself on a Greek island while you were up in——' grey eyes locked directly into hers '—Warwickshire, wasn't it?'

'That's right.'

'Where else to retire to than a secluded old English inn deep in the old English countryside?' he remarked laconically. 'As hideaways go, they don't come better.'

'I wasn't away long,' Keri protested. 'You must only just have missed me.'

'After the trauma of your father dying, you felt you were in line for a break?' Warily she nodded. 'And did tramping the meadows, knocking your head on low oak beams, wallowing in a surfeit of mulled wine and venison prove to be therapeutic?'

She nodded again, unhappy to be force fed with such a sarcastic scenario. Shafe made it sound as though her time in Warwickshire had been not only self-indulgent and unnecessary, but less than legitimate. She understood how galling his two wasted journeys must have been, but this attack was unfair.

'I'm sorry your ring on the doorbell went unanswered,' she said, 'but how can you expect a brass band and cheer leaders waiting if you fail to give warning you're about to drop by? Regrettably, telepathy didn't feature on the curriculum at my school.'

'So I discovered. But you enjoyed yourself in Warwickshire?' he insisted.

'A change of scene was...invigorating.'

'I can imagine,' he said thinly.

Keri frowned. During subsequent telephone calls she had made no mention of the visit—neither had he of his, she thought with a flash of irritation— but it was no secret. On the contrary, she had been hoarding a report with the intention of producing it with a flourish as evidence that as he was willing to alter his way of life so she, too, was making adjustments. The news represented a gift, a kind of peace offering. Had he been more amenable there would have been a prompt presentation, instead she decided to keep her exposé until later.

'You had good weather?' he enquired.

'Rotten. It poured from the moment I arrived until the moment I left. I never went anywhere without my umbrella.'

News of the incessant rain blatantly appealed, and when Shafe next spoke his abrasive tone had been replaced by jokiness. 'In Barbados all you'll need is a bikini, the itsier-bitsier the better.'

'I've brought one or two,' she said. 'For me, and for Emma.'

'This hussy wears a bikini?' he teased, lifting the toddler from her.

'Just the bottom half.'

His grey eyes swept over Keri, efficiently removing every stitch of her clothing.

'And how about you, toots? Do you intend to follow suit? Personally I'd prefer you to be my very own centrefold, but——'

'I doubt she'll sit in that,' Keri interrupted as he placed Emma in the car seat, but once again she was proved wrong. Instead of throwing a rigid-legged fit, her daughter benignly allowed herself to be strapped in among the gear.

Minutes later they left the airport, driving through a warm, heady evening which pulsated with the sonorous bleeps of singing frogs and crickets. In comparison with most girls of twenty-six, Keri was widely travelled, yet even so this first taste of the Caribbean had her captivated. Maybe the roads were pockmarked with holes, maybe most of the houses resembled pastel-painted garden huts, shabby ones at that. But the air was fragrant, hibiscus grew, and whenever the highway touched the coast there came the soft crash of waves on a shore she could not see, yet which she knew would be the paradise the travel brochures depicted. Roll on tomorrow, when she would be rested and could admire everything in daylight.

'Why did you suggest we meet up here?' she enquired curiously, as they sped along.

Shafe hissed out a breath. 'I didn't figure on New York being conducive. Granted, our apartment's comfortable, but the setting seemed too...

mundane. Besides, if my mother had got wind of her granddaughter being within striking distance, she'd have broken the door down. Mom's a sweetheart, but she's always had a tendency to think she can run my life better than me. I didn't want her trying to dabble in our affairs.' He moved his shoulders. 'As for London——'

'Angela?'

'Bull's eye. This damned Yank didn't need his sister-in-law poking her nose in, either. Tell me, I realise something about her vacation must have failed to meet with approval, but what? Was the island the wrong shape? The ouzo too cheap? The Aegean half a degree too warm? Or maybe she took a strong aversion to the locals?'

'On the contrary, she liked them, or at least she liked one. Ever since she arrived home she's been drooling over photographs of herself entwined with some raven-headed Mr Machismo. What's more, she's phoned him twice and writes almost every day.'

'You mean there's a guy alive whom Angela rates higher than something nasty she's stepped in?'

Keri grinned. 'You can be crude.'

'It's a gift.'

'I accept New York and London had their drawbacks, but did you have any special reason for choosing Barbados?' she asked, returning to her original question.

'No.' He pursed his lips, hesitating for a moment. 'Though——' Ahead a small, long-tailed animal streaked out from a clump of bamboo. 'Jeez!' he exclaimed, and stamped on the brake.

'What was that?'

'A mongoose. A century or two ago they were introduced to kill off the snakes and it worked, the island's snake-free. Problem is,' he added drily, 'now the place supports a thriving community of mongooses...Mongeese? OK, ragtag?' he enquired, as a gabble came from behind, but Emma had regarded the emergency stop as a special event laid on for her benefit and was smacking delighted hands. 'Good thing she was strapped in tight. I meant to tell you,' Shafe said, as they resumed their journey, 'I've organised a cot, a high chair, a baby alarm system. Also there's a gate in the fence which separates the garden from the shore, but you don't need to worry because it's been fitted with a child-proof bolt.'

Keri's sideways look held a mixture of appreciation and pithy scorn. Had he become the concerned parent? Remarkable, considering the occasions he had found time to play such a role previously were rare to the point of novelty.

'The hotel's been very obliging.'

'We're not booked into a hotel.' All of a sudden the road ahead demanded his full concentration. 'We're staying in one of my father's properties.'

Her brows rose. She knew her father-in-law would never have risked offering accommodation, not after being turned down so often, which meant Shafe must have made the first move.

'He squeezed us in at short notice?' she enquired, keeping her voice neutral.

'He did,' came the curt reply.

Keri suppressed a smile. The senior Mr Rokeby, a man of prodigious energy, like his son, owned a company which rented out holiday villas and apartments at prime locations throughout the States and West Indies. Justifiably proud, his long-held hope was for the business to become a family dynasty. Harris, his elder son, had complied, but Shafe fought against nepotism tooth and nail. Not only had the idea of working alongside his father been rejected, but any form of what he classed as 'handouts' had been declared taboo. He did things his way, alone.

'It made Pop happy,' he continued, prickly and defensive. 'Besides, I've recently gotten to thinking how I'd like Emma to benefit from any success of mine. Don't get me wrong, I want her to be independent, but I'd be hurt if she turned her back and said no thanks to *everything*. Ideas change,' he muttered, losing patience with himself, 'people change.'

'You?'

The enquiry had been light, but all of a sudden Keri discovered it was a loaded question, one which demanded she hold her breath.

'I guess.' He laughed, turning it into a joke. 'Not only is there this——' he ran his thumb along his top lip '—but for the first time in history I'm embarking on a lengthy vacation.'

A lengthy vacation. Keri savoured the phrase, her mouth moving into a smile as she dwelt on the blissful prospect and the attendant connotations.

'And do you realise it's a unique event in our history, too?' she asked. 'That in all the time we've known each other, we've never been together for six completely uninterrupted weeks?'

'Indeed I do.'

Her smile was wiped out. She had heard caution in his voice, only a tinge, but sufficient to put her on the alert. There was something about those 'six completely uninterrupted weeks' which made him uneasy. Could Shafe be wondering if fixing such a span had been rash to the point of foolishness? Was he having second thoughts; not about them being together, but about how he would fill his time once the talking had been accomplished? A career which sent him hurtling from one country to the next, invariably to areas of high tension, allowed few breaks in which to develop hobbies, though he was not the growing dahlias, gone fishing kind of man. On the contrary, he was, as the psychology jargon put it, a Type A—dynamic and goal-orientated. And possessed of a low boredom threshold. Would he be able to unwind or instead grow fractious and edgy? Keri was about to begin detailing the joys of sunning, swimming and sailing, when he swung off the highway on to a gravelled drive lined with stately Royal palms.

'Our destination,' he grinned.

They had arrived at a low, white bungalow with a porch covered in purple bougainvillaea and a front door which opened quickly.

'May I introduce Suzette Scatterberry,' he said, as a wand-slim black woman in her late thirties came to greet them. 'She looks after the house, does the washing, prepares the food.' He winked conspiratorially at the beaming housekeeper. 'Even better, she's let me in on the secret of how to make rum punch Barbadian-style.'

Suzette chuckled and welcomed Keri to the island. 'This is your darling daughter?' she asked, when she caught sight of Emma. 'Aw, honey, Victor's gonna love you.'

'Who's Victor?' Keri asked, unbuckling the solemn-eyed toddler as Shafe began to unload the moke.

'My youngest. He's three. He'll be around tomorrow.' A slender hand indicated the bungalow. 'While the boss is busy, suppose I show you around?'

The accommodation was compact but luxurious, comprising two bedrooms each with en-suite bathroom, a well equipped kitchen and a white carpeted living-room/dinette which opened out on to a patio at the rear. The patio, a marble-floored expanse stretching the entire width of the bungalow, contained rattan armchairs and loungers upholstered in a floral chintz. A smooth lawn rolled down to a picket fence, and beyond it moonlight silvered a line of tall casuarinas mingled with what Suzette identified as geranium trees.

'Behind them's the shore. This stretch is called the Platinum Coast, because of the brilliant white of the sand. I usually arrive around nine and leave after serving dinner early evening, with a three-hour break in the afternoons,' she explained, as they walked back to the front of the house, 'but if you want me to come in earlier, stay later, maybe baby-sit, just you let me know.'

'Thanks. When we're organised, I will.'

'Look like some rum punch'd go down real fine right now,' the woman grinned, as Shafe deposited the last piece of luggage indoors and wiped a glistening brow. 'Supposin' I mix a jugful before I say goodnight and leave it on a tray with a couple of glasses?'

'Just one glass, thanks,' Keri said, pressing down a hand on the top of her head. 'Jet lag's hit, so anything alcoholic would knock me flat on my back.'

'Then how's about a cup of coffee and a bite to eat?'

'Lovely, and while you're doing that I'll dispose of the enemy.' She hugged the toddler in her arms. 'A swift top and tail, a bottle of juice, and into the Land of Nod. And if you're not asleep in two seconds flat, Mummy'll murder you.'

Twenty minutes later, Shafe poked his head around the door of the smaller of the two bedrooms and grinned. Emma was rollicking around the cot, chirpy as a kewpie doll.

'Looks like it's time to remove all the blunt instruments.'

Keri groaned. 'Do it quickly.'

He came forward. 'Honey, your coffee and sandwiches are waiting in the living-room. Go through and leave this young madam to me.'

What a relief it was to obey, and after something to eat and drink she felt better; not so much revived as wearily content. Shafe, by the fervour of his kiss at the airport, had fulfilled her predictions. He continued to love her. His desire remained as strong as ever. Wrong there, Angela! Her sister had repeatedly muttered about the rendezvous being 'make or break time, only delete the make', but her grasp of the basics were faulty. Granted, a goodly proportion of their two-year marriage had been conducted with him in one hemisphere and her in another, but it was a case of knocking the relationship into shape, not termination. She did not want to end anything—heaven forbid!—and neither did Shafe.

Keri nestled down in the corner of the sofa. At thirty-four, her husband had enjoyed a longer than average run of the free-wheeling life, so although he might not be delirious about its demise he could have no grounds for complaint. After all, no one could do exactly what they wanted for ever and a day. Limitations must be accepted, adjustments undertaken. And once Shafe kicked the habit of disappearing at a moment's notice, cut loose from a life which was all whistle and no stop, then they could settle down to some prime-time living. She wound a strand of ash-blonde hair around her finger, contentedly mulling over what lay ahead. Shafe settled in his new job and the apartment sold, they would move to a house with a garden within commuting distance of the New York studios. She had already set her heart on a neighbourhood—one Shafe admired for its understated elegance and wide range of amenities—and already hankered after a particular avenue lined with cherry blossom trees. The house—Keri had it furnished in her mind's eye—would be light and airy and comfortable. Green, gold and white would be the colour scheme. There would be a rumpus room, a spacious lounge, a study for Shafe. Her thoughts quickened. One of the bedrooms—they would need four—would be a nursery, because after a year or two they would have a second child. It would be a planned pregnancy next time, and——

'That's one of the goldilockses in my life out for the count. Now the other looks like she could use some shut-eye,' remarked a bourbon-brown voice.

'Emma's asleep? However did you manage that?'

'I'd bought her a mobile, so I fixed it up and it twirled and glittered, and hypnotised her.' Shafe jerked his head towards a cupboard. 'There are enough goodies hidden away in there to fill a toy shop. I was planning to dole them out one at a time.' He paused, giving her a long, cool look. 'Unless you have any objections?'

'None.'

On the contrary, Keri was delighted. Considering the generous and imaginative gifts he had given her, his track record where buying presents for their daughter was concerned left much to be desired.

He walked to the bar which formed a divider from the dining area. 'Do you remember Joseph Harewood?' he asked, pouring himself a glass of punch.

'Joey?' She gave a laugh of surprise. 'Of course. Why?'

'Just that you'll be seeing him again.'

'Here, in Barbados?'

'That's right. He might be a multi-millionaire controlling a multi-million-dollar business, but he never forgets those further down the line. Every year he pays for some of the guys who hold franchises for his swimming pools to take their families on vacation. Joey and his wife organise a swanky hotel and a full programme. One of the highlights is an all day party on the *Bajan Buccaneer*. That's where you'll be meeting him. The *Buccaneer*'s a tall-masted schooner,' he explained. 'It sails out from Bridgetown and up the coast with a steel band on board. After drinks and a steak lunch, time's allowed for snorkelling, swimming, a trip in a glass-bottom boat, that kind of thing.'

'Sounds great.' Puzzled, Keri tilted her head. 'I take it you've seen Joey and he's invited us?'

'Yup, but——' Shafe frowned down into his drink, then looked up. 'I'm fudging the issue. It isn't simply you and me joining him for a day out. There's a camera crew going aboard and I'll be tied up with filming for a while.'

'Filming?' she echoed in disbelief.

'I'm doing a profile on Joey. It's a one-off,' he said, when she sat bolt upright. 'I've interviewed the guy in New York—remember how his office overlooks Central Park?—spoken to his employees at a couple of depots, been to his home, and now——'

'And now you're in Barbados to damn well work!' She leapt to her feet. 'I thought you'd arranged to come here because you needed to talk to me, because you wanted to renew your acquaintance with Emma, because——' she flung at him '—the two goldilockses in your life *mattered*. Oh no, we were tossed in as a side issue!'

'That's not true.'

Keri glared. Everything that held any meaning—the reorganisation of their marriage, her future happiness, the emotional security of their child—had hinged on these gloriously free six weeks, weeks she believed he had devoted to *her*. She had taken them to be a pledge, a guarantee of his good intent, and here he was tearing them up, tearing strips off their relationship, tearing her apart.

'Ever since I've known you, your career's come first,' she spat, allowing her anger full rein, because if she didn't the treacherous sting of tears warned she might break down and cry. 'I understood we were to spend time together and talk, but what do I find?—you tooled for action, while

Emma and I are fitted in around a television schedule!'

'You're not being fitted in around anything. As for my career, sure you don't like us being apart and I don't like it either—not that the separation these past few months has been my fault,' he slid in curtly, 'but you've always gone along with it.'

'What you mean is, I've never made any waves.'

'I wasn't aware you wanted to.'

'A married man has a duty to be home at nights, instead of gallivanting around the world with never a care.'

Shafe took a swig of his drink. 'Amazing, your lips move and I hear Angela's voice coming out.'

'Bastard! I should have guessed Barbados wasn't a lucky dip choice, that you had to have some other motive for making the trip. And I should have known from the shady look on your face when I mentioned six completely uninterrupted weeks that it was a sham.'

A nerve throbbed in his temple. 'All the Joey connection entails is checking out the boat and doing the interview at the end of our stay. I'll be involved for two or three days at most, which leaves plenty of time for us to——'

'Us? Huh!'

'OK, maybe I could be accused of not putting enough into our marriage in the past, but there are reasons.' Receiving no response, he sighed. 'We all need to make a living, Keri, and as I remember it you were pretty keen on your career yourself once. Did I demand you cook me a three-course meal every evening, or provide constant fresh shirts, or cancel an assignment if it coincided with some of my free time?' Still she remained silent. 'Honey, I happen to be a television reporter who travels the globe.'

'A reporter is not what you happen to be, it's what you *do*,' Keri said fiercely. 'You happen to *be* a husband and father.'

A spread of his hands conceded the error. 'And in those categories I haven't won prizes?'

'Not so far.'

'If you've stuck with me this long, I must be doing something right.' He gave a lopsided smile. 'Mustn't I?'

'Like what?' she snapped.

Shafe's smile switched off. 'Will you stop making me the heavy here? Has it never struck you that if things are screwed up, I didn't do it all on my own?' For a moment his eyes were like cold unreachable marbles, then he shifted his stance. 'Haven't we butted our heads together long enough?' he appealed. 'I'd like to pack in this argument and, if you're honest, I'm sure you would, too. Coping with a small child on a lengthy plane journey can't have been easy. You look worn out.'

She needed to clench her fists to keep from hitting him. Her head ached, her stomach was pitching and tossing, and she felt dizzy with fatigue, but how dared he slither out of the wrong and wind up criticising *her*?

'I assure you I'm fine,' she replied, as icily superior as she could make it.

'Yes, ma'am.' That lopsided smile was tugging at the corner of Shafe's mouth again. 'But you'll feel much finer—and so will I—after a good night's sleep. Why not come to bed?'

She stared at him. He—the villain who had shot her coveted six weeks through with so many holes you could use them to drain spaghetti—now expected her to lie meekly by his side? Come to bed, she knew what that meant. Agreed, Shafe never pushed, but there was no need. All he had to do was murmur his desire and kiss her and stroke her breasts, and, tired or not, before she knew it she would be aflame. She might even find herself begging him to make love to her! It had happened before.

Keri stalked across to her daughter's room. On the threshold, she paused. There was a moment when her eyes fired a volley of poison-tipped arrows, then she flung open the door and stepped inside.

'Go to hell!' she rasped, and extravagantly slammed the door shut.

CHAPTER TWO

As DRAMATIC exits went it excelled, but Keri's satisfaction had lasted a minuscule ten seconds—the time it took Emma to awaken. Being yanked from sleep by a loud noise to find yourself in a strange cot, in a strange room, with a pale and fraught mother who is more concerned with her own problems than yours, is enough to make anyone cry. Emma cried. Emma sobbed. Emma's chest heaved beneath the row of gingham bunnies appliquéd to her nightdress. Emma's nose ran.

Wielding tissues, Keri held her close and twirled the stupid mobile and wished her husband would appear to work one of his miracles. No, she didn't. She would rather her daughter cried the entire night than be comforted by *him*. All the same, just because she'd said to go to hell it didn't mean he couldn't tap on the door and enquire if there was anything he could do; that would be no more than common decency. But Shafe kept himself to himself.

Emma's howling in memory of the unhappy awakening went on and on. The din would have stopped a deaf man from falling asleep, yet when the child finally calmed down and she walked her across the floor in an attempt to settle her off again, Keri had a sneaky suspicion a snore might have emanated from the bedroom through the wall. On the other hand, she thought, as her eyes narrowed into slits, it could be Shafe teasing. He possessed

28

an oddball and, at times, totally inappropriate sense of humour. Settling Emma off proved even trickier than stopping her from crying. In the end Keri admitted defeat. She switched off the light, lay down on the bed alongside the cot, and watched the toddler play. First one of the long-suffering Baxter's flippers were chewed, then a moonbeam caught her interest, next—— Somewhere along the way, Keri fell asleep. In time her daughter fell asleep, too. There was a brief, fuzzy, stumbling moment in the depths of the night when she covered the child—for the room was air-conditioned cool—then she peeled off her clothes, slid between the sheets and crashed out again. The next time she awoke the sun shone golden behind heavy white lace curtains, and the cot beside her lay empty.

Keri stretched, then sighed as her mind flew back to the previous evening. Any outsider listening to her outburst would accuse her of being excessively nit-picking. Irrational, almost. Chop a couple of days out of six weeks and did you wind up with a disaster? Most would say no and they would be right, but they missed the point. That lay in the television programme being the *real* reason why Shafe had come to Barbados. Their time together might be the lion's share, but what was the betting its place in the sequence of events had been second? She resented being subsequent. It hurt. It negated, it sullied her dreams.

Somehow, in a calm, mature way, she must express that resentment. Last night, admittedly, she had been in a frenzy, but the outburst was atypical—tiredness had caused everything to mushroom. Equally, whining and grumbles were not her style either, though now Keri wondered whether, in the past, she had fallen into the trap of being too obliging. Should she have voiced more complaints? Her sister would have scored there. Angela had honed being positively negative into an art form. Ah well, too late to backtrack and become one of nature's dissidents. Besides, the truth was she had been so busy with Emma that, for a long time, she had never noticed anything lacking in their marriage, and later exactly how much. It was only during their elongated separation that she had become aware of a growing dissatisfaction.

Keri gazed at the ceiling. Last night had clarified her feelings, put them into sharp relief. Now she felt indignant, deprived and in no mood to be messed around. Never mind waiting until Shafe deigned to talk turkey. At the first opportunity he would be informed that where changes in their lives were concerned, her turn had come to call the shots!

'Wonder what time it is,' she muttered, reaching across to bat a hand unproductively over the bedside table in search of her watch.

'One o'clock,' Shafe said, strolling in a moment later.

Startled, she gazed up at him. 'You heard me?'

'I was next door, changing, and I used the baby alarm to check if you were awake. Had a good sleep?'

'Excellent, once I managed it,' she replied with a glower, then hastily switched from hanging half out of bed to sitting up, tucking the sheet under her armpits. What Shafe had changed into were his swimming trunks, brief stretchy white ones, and him being well on the way to nakedness was a sharp reminder that she was fully so. Why nudity should become a problem instead of the usual delight she did not know, but it had. Perhaps because her husband continued to remind her of an alien? 'It was good of you to install an alarm,' she said briskly, 'though in actual fact I no longer use one.'

'You close the door and leave Emma to her own devices? Alleluia! In New York every breath she took needed to be monitored.'

'She was much younger,' Keri defended, 'and you used to listen, too.'

'Only when she was very new. I soon realised the kid was blessed with sufficient lung power to call for help, as she demonstrated last night,' he said, a wry brow arched.

'Where did you pick up the tan?' she enquired, indicating her disdain on *that* subject by refusing to respond.

Lithe and bronzed and glowing with good health, Shafe looked as if he should be promoting jet-set aperitifs or expensive sports cars. Pathetically, Keri found herself mesmerised by the gleam of his skin.

'In Beirut.' Fingertips were rubbed among the golden hairs on his chest. 'I spent a couple of days there last week, so this comes courtesy of the Lebanese sun.'

'You never said on the phone that you were going,' she protested, feeling woefully undermined. Once he had shared everything with her; suddenly there were too many gaps. 'Or that you'd been.'

'It was a rush job. I saw no reason to worry you.'

The reply was matter-of-fact, but a shadow of something hard to label—distaste? strain?—crossed his face.

'You felt as uncomfortable with the place this time as you did last time?'

'You remember the last time?'

'In detail. Emma must have been around six months old, and when you came home you were ... uptight. That had been a rush job too, an in-and-out trip of a few days, yet it took ages before you were properly relaxed again.'

'Never thought you'd noticed.' His words were an accusation, one which forced Keri into a swerve.

'Any chance of something to eat? I'm starving.'

'Suzette's setting out lunch right now.'

'Great. I'll shower and be ready in less than five minutes.'

'You're going to risk getting out of bed while I'm in the room?' he drawled. 'My God!'

Secretly she had been thinking along the lines of a rapid dash into the bathroom with the idea that he might have gone when she emerged, but now it became imperative to lock into his cold, objective gaze and stare it down.

'I don't know what you're talking about,' Keri declared, tossing a shiny strand of hair from her shoulder.

'Yes, you do. I'd barely walked through the door before you started acting like you were a virgin and I was a highwayman hell-bent on ravishment.' Shafe had become sprung steel. 'You may not be a virgin, you honoured me with that gift many moons ago, but I *am* hell-bent on ravishment. And why not? The last occasion when I sated my lust, as the saying goes, was during the week I spent in London to attend your father's funeral. As you were grieving, Emma had teething troubles, and the sharp-eared Angela inhabited the room across the hall, the occasion was not one calculated to allow full expression of marital bliss. Set that apart, and for the last four months or so I've gone to bed sober, early and alone. In these days of marital infidelity maybe it's unusual, but I happen to be one of the guys who takes no interest in extraneous females, not even those of an inflatable nature.' He took a step forward. 'Which means that when my wife is with me I want to make love to her—hard and long and frequently. Which also means——' he came closer '—that while you may have derived some satisfaction from spending last night on your own, it did nothing for me. So be warned, engineering an argument in order to flounce off like a prima donna won't work a second time.'

'I didn't engineer an argument!'

'You didn't flounce off, either? Oh, but you did, lady, and it bugged the living hell out of me, though I'm trying to rise above it. Do you know how often I've imagined how last night would be? How I longed to be able to reach out in the dark and feel you warm and soft beside me? How much I wanted to wake up with a woman, the woman being my wife, *you*?'

Keri looked at her hands. 'I over-reacted.'

'And how! We're only together five minutes before you decide to blow off steam and slam doors.'

'I wasn't blowing off steam. OK, I was,' she muttered, when he raised disbelieving brows. 'But I was also making a legitimate observation. There comes a time in everyone's life when they must concede——' A yell from the garden had her starting forward. 'Someone needs to be rescued.'

'You stay where you are.' His voice had gained a cutting edge. 'Talking to your husband takes precedence over mollycoddling a child who deserves all she gets. Ever since Victor arrived she's been trying her best to boss him around. The little guy might be two years older and four inches taller, but he's needing to fight your daughter every step of the way. If he's knocked her down, it's about time.'

'He hasn't. That's not her squealing, it must be him. And Emma's your daughter, too.'

'When the chin goes up and she weighs into a poor, unsuspecting male, she's pure Momma's girl.' He dropped down on the bed beside her, and as his grey eyes fell she realised the sheet had also fallen. 'Why is it when I look at you I forget thirty-six inches are only a goddamn yard?' he demanded.

Exposed to his gaze, a devouring gaze, Keri felt a strange mixture of embarrassment and arousal. The alien aspect of the moustachioed Shafe made her want to shy away, yet there was enough of the 'familiar' Shafe to bring hot memories of their previous lovemaking to mind.

'You gave Emma her breakfast this morning?' she queried. She longed to cover herself up, but balked at renewed 'virgin' accusations.

'Yup. After bathing her and dressing her.'

'You did all that?'

He nodded. 'I thought it was time I had a try.'

'And what did Emma think?'

'That it was odd. In particular, she wasn't amused when I almost strangled her putting her dress over her head, though all was forgiven when I demonstrated a flair of Donald Duck noises. Now, about you and me making——'

'What did she have to eat?'

'Bananas, and stop changing the subject.'

'She doesn't like bananas. She usually spits them out.'

'Not for me, she doesn't.'

'But——'

'Keri, put a lid on it. Please!' Long, tanned fingers enclosed a full ripe curve, its tip nudging into his palm. 'You have the most beautiful breasts, skin made of satin——' his hand slid beneath the sheet, his thumb searching, finding, rubbing until she gasped '—and crevices which are so moist, so sweet, the thought of them is driving me crazy.' The harsh tone of a moment ago had softened to become almost a purr. 'Mrs Rokeby, I want to lick you, all of you. Now.'

'Shafe, we can't,' she protested, her heart thundering as she recognised the look of raw need in his eyes. 'The door's open, lunch is almost ready, and——'

Steering her back against the pillow, he stopped her protest with a kiss. And another and another. And as he fondled, caressed, rolled the knubs of her breasts between a thumb and a forefinger, a drugging cloud of desire encompassed her. Keri wound her arms around his neck and whimpered. Her brain was pushing for no, insisting this was neither the time nor the place, but her emotions were arguing a different case. Let him love you. Why not, when you want him as much as he wants you? Yes. Yes. Please. For far too long she had been without him and now all that mattered was his mouth on hers, the insistent pleasure of his hands, the pressure of the hard, lean length of his body.

'Honey, you don't know how much I've missed you. How many nights I've lain awake thinking about you, imagining touching you and the way you touch me.' His moustache tantalised as he nuzzled his head into the blonde tumble of her hair. 'Why don't those beautiful hands of yours walk down to my hips and peel away my——' He broke off to dispense a mouthful of asterisk-speckled abuse. Suzette was announcing that lunch was ready. 'Soon,' he called, before once more pressing his lips to her neck where he kissed and nibbled the warm skin. 'After all this celibacy, I'm expected to rate eating shrimp as superior to eating you? No way. What's the matter?' he asked, as her body tensed.

'I can hear the patter of tiny feet.'

The abuse became murderous imprecations as infant giggles warned of imminent disruption.

'You haven't programmed Emma to do this?' he demanded, as he stood up. If he had meant it as a joke, it did not sound like one. 'What time does she go to bed these days?'

'Around seven-thirty.'

'I guess I have no choice than to wait until then, but at thirty-one minutes past you and I have a date. Making love. Thick and fast, followed by slow and long, for twelve hours solid. And——' Shafe's jaw jutted like a granite buttress '—I won't be taking no for an answer.'

'Then yes.'

Keri's bright smile masked a pang of uncertainty. If she could be accused of excessive behaviour last night, wasn't he guilty now? This harsh determination smacked of the extreme. Anyone would think she had sworn to withhold her favours for ever and a day, when all she had done was stomp off in a temper.

He rewarded her with a grin and a reconciliation, of sorts. 'Should the need to let off more steam hit, do us both a favour and hold back. You might feel fine right now, but you're still jet lagged and so am I. The Lebanon trip involved a couple of long-haul flights from which I've yet to recover, so I'd be grateful if we could postpone any——' his accent became a super de luxe American drawl '—meaningful discussions. Today we eat, drink, lie in the sun, and there's no pressure. Agreed?'

Keri frowned. Could discussing the future—making it plain she was a force to be reckoned with—wait another twenty-four hours? Should it wait?

'Maamee! Dadda!'

Emma and her sidekick had arrived.

She laughed. 'Agreed.'

What they ate were jumbo prawns, served in a spicy cream sauce on a bed of salad. What they drank was ice-cold Banks beer, the brew of Barbados. After lunch Suzette made ready to whisk Victor off but, displaying a definite bent towards masochism, so Shafe remarked, the little boy begged to be allowed to stay with his new girlfriend. This was agreed, and as his mother disappeared Shafe and Keri shepherded the two toddlers out through the fence, weighed down with sufficient stores to equip an army.

At first Emma, wearing frilly bloomers, lashings of sun oil and a floppy hat, did not trust the waves, but Victor plopping down at the water's edge was a challenge she could not resist. Ker-plunk! Bravely she went down on her bottom, splashing him, her father and herself. There was a moment when a lip quivered, then she gave a wide melon smile. The Caribbean had passed muster.

Marvelling at sea shells came next, followed by being forcibly restrained from shoving ropes of lime-green seaweed into her mouth. Later everyone retired to the shade of a huge tamarind tree and, as Shafe began work on a sandcastle while the children supplied their own dubious brand of assistance, Keri examined the scene. Her photographer's eye had never seen such colours. Take shots, and who back home would believe the whiteness of the spun sugar sand, the sky's magical blue, the turquoise of a sea which darkened into a pencil line of navy at the horizon?

'Yeah, man,' cried a youth, provoked into cabaret by his Walkman.

As he sauntered past, snapping his fingers and giving stray hip glides, her gaze followed. Lazily he went along the arc of shore to where half a dozen catamarans had been beached. Sails of yellow, pink and orange flapped in the breeze and jib forestays clattered. Add the sighing of palms, and a seaside concerto was created.

Suddenly she became aware of Shafe looking at her. His gaze, like the accompanying comment about his castle being under threat from infant demolition experts, was outwardly casual, yet Keri sensed herself to be under intense observation. He seemed restless and aloof. Why? Did fury at having slept alone continue to simmer—despite acting the devoted father, the tension which radiated from him had never allowed her to forget for one moment that he regarded himself as the defrauded lover— or was jet lag and the Lebanon taking its toll? His visit would have been no pleasure trip. Anything but. In the background of the first broadcast she had heard gunfire, yet when he returned home her dismay had received short shrift. Yes, snipers lurked on every corner and bombs were detonated daily, but he saw no point in dwelling on them. And since then the situation in that strife-torn country had worsened.

Keri rolled over on to her stomach. Maybe her surmisings were off-target and his distraction could be attributed to the forthcoming television profile? That would make more sense, she thought pungently. Whatever Shafe did he concentrated on it with all his power, which was formidable. Having begun his career as a political journalist, his knowledge of the government of his own country and many others meant that writing his own scripts came easy, but even so every question was backed by painstaking research. Nothing in his sometimes sympathetic, sometimes remorseless probing of people in the news was left to chance. Maybe the Joseph Harewood profile could be construed as lightweight compared to international emergencies, yet there had to be huge gouts of interest hidden among the rags-to-riches success. Keri trickled a handful of sand through her fingers. Shafe's involvement was supposed to take up three days at maximum, but that reference covered the practicalities, not thinking time. Let's eat, drink and lie in the sun, he had pleaded, depicting an 'easy does it' philosophy, yet here he was in the grip of mental machinations!

She rested her head on her arms. If he had spoken with Joey several times already, shouldn't matters be cut and dried? Unlike the political fraternity, the millionaire did not evade the issue nor act the clam. On the contrary, he was open and straight-

forward. Joseph Harewood, she thought drowsily—
a most unlikely Cupid.

Whenever Larry Roach, Keri's boss and features
editor of the quality newspaper, the *Enquirer*, came
up with an idea, he wasted no time in putting it
into action. Which was how, at twenty-four hours'
notice, she had found herself flying to the States.
A colour supplement spread, which contrasted the
life-styles of three leading businessmen needed
photographs, and she was required to point her lens
at a Japanese microchip wizard, an English
property magnate and Joseph Harewood. Larry's
confidence in her talents had swiftly turned her into
the paper's youngest roving photographer, and this
all-expenses-paid trip was a good omen for the
future; though in the event a crackshot television
man turned her future inside out and upside down.

An observation by the millionaire on a recent
hiccup on Wall Street had taken longer to film than
expected, and as Keri's eagerness to be punctual
had resulted in her arriving early at the suite of offices, she and Shafe had severely overlapped. For
him it had been instant attraction. Her long blonde
hair, alert blue eyes and streamlined body fitted into
pink satin bomber jacket and baggy trousers had
seen to that. His outfit of city-smart suit, subdued
shirt, neat knotted tie, had had the reverse effect.
She had taken him to be a mainstream 'yuppie'—
a young, urban professional—and although she
didn't have anything against such men, the first
impression was of someone narrowly channelled.
A touch of devilment in his smile, however, had
hinted otherwise, so when he had suggested dinner,
she had found herself accepting. Shafe joining her

in denim shirt and blue jeans, with a crusty leather jacket slung on top, had altered her perceptions.

He was, Keri soon discovered, a man of many parts. Canny enough to subtly alter his persona to suit the subject under interview, he could be light-heartedly anonymous, fierce and leonine, a solid shape with a savvy mind. With Joseph Harewood, he had been the latter. Keeping your wits about you was vital in the millionaire's company. A five-foot barrel of a man who must have been made when they'd run out of necks, Joey warmed to a biting reply, an apt comment. He had warmed to Keri, and been delighted with the photographs she had taken of him. It would be nice to meet him again, she mused. Nicer still if the occasion hadn't been brought about by *business*!

After an all too brief session of getting to know Shafe in New York, an ocean had intervened. Four weeks later riots in West Germany had occurred and he had fortuitously been despatched to cover them. The flight from Munich to London was short. Fleeting and intermittent meetings had followed, snatched where and whenever possible: two days in Vienna, a long weekend outside Rome, a reunion beside Lake Geneva. Over the months there were more trysts, interspersed by phone calls and sheafs of letters. Come summer, Keri had flown west and they had spent three weeks in Shafe's New Jersey apartment, surfacing only to check whether it was day or night and buy an occasional bag of groceries. That time together had changed everything. The chemistry became alchemy. Neither of them had been planning on getting married, but both had realised that meeting the other, being with the other, *loving* the other, was totally different from everything which had gone before.

Keri had resigned from the newspaper, arranged for her belongings to be shipped to the States and, almost a year from their first meeting, they walked down the aisle as man and wife. Switzerland was chosen for their honeymoon. Here, among the mountains and lakes, Anglo-American relations had been continually and rapturously cemented, and their daughter had been conceived.

Thoughts of Emma drew her back to the present. Too much tropical sun too soon must be avoided, and she sat up to check the little girl remained in the shade. Keri grinned. Not only was her daughter curled up beneath the tree, but Victor and Shafe lay alongside. All three had their eyes closed. The exhaustion of castle building, she thought, mentally naming the scene. What a pity her camera had been left in the bungalow. Never mind, another time. She searched in her beach bag for oil. Emma needed no attention, but another fifteen minutes would get her own tan off to a good start.

'Let me,' Shafe said, commandeering the bottle.

'I thought you were asleep.'

'What chance have I of sleeping when you're less than six feet away, full of breast, slim of waist, and wearing damn all?' he retorted brusquely. 'Lie down.'

The hands which oiled her back were strong and sure, and evocative. From shoulder to hip he rubbed, so smoothly, so sensuously, that her skin tingled and an ache began to gnaw. She recalled those halcyon days wandering through flower-strewn fields high above Interlaken, starry nights in New Jersey, the passion and perfection, the sheer lunacy of being in love. Everything had seemed so simple then. Keri moved uneasily. She itched. She throbbed. She felt open and exposed. It was as if his fingers were massaging not only her body, but her thoughts, her emotions, her very soul.

'Relax,' he murmured.

Unable to bear his touch a moment longer without succumbing to *something*, she twisted from lying on her stomach to resting back on her elbows.

'How about you relaxing?' she challenged.

Shafe's eyes darkened into storm clouds of grey. 'There's only one thing which'll relax me, and you know what that is.' He stretched out a hand and dragged a fingertip slowly across her ribcage. 'Suzette'll be back soon, so why don't we ask her to mind the kids while we go inside, take off our clothes, and——'

'You folks gettin' along OK?' grinned a tall black youth wearing ragged jeans and a bright knitted woollen cap over a mop of bulging dreadlocks. 'Captain Smiley at your service, come to show you my jewellery store.'

Muttering something grisly about enticement to strangulation, Shafe rolled from her and sat up.

'We've only just arrived,' he replied, as a briefcase was opened and coral necklaces and bracelets displayed. 'Perhaps tomorrow?'

'You new here, chief? Fantastic! Captain Smiley can give you de inside knowledge on places to eat, to swim, to buy souvenirs.'

'Tomorrow?' Shafe pleaded again, but the youth proved unstoppable.

He also proved to be lousy with charm, which meant any initial reluctance to become involved was quickly dissipated and they were soon planning sightseeing tours, deciding which beaches to explore, discussing where they might perhaps dine.

'Just mention my name,' he was saying much later, as he fastened his case and made to depart. 'Everyone knows Captain Smiley, and Captain Smiley knows everyone.'

'Baz Guiler?' Keri enquired.

'Don't 'xactly *know* de guy, but I hear de tales.'

'Can you tell me where he lives?'

'St Philips, that's a parish over on the east. Get yourself on de coast road and take de second turn, after Ginger Bay. Can't give specifics like name and number of de street, 'cos de guy don't advertise, but he's there somewhere. He's become a hermit. Odd, him being de big man on the rock scene—I mean real big, big like Texas—and all those chicks goin' mad for him——' He stopped short, his dark eyes touring speculatively over her curves in the yellow bikini. 'Not one of dem, are you?'

A guffaw came from Shafe's direction. 'Mad about a jerk who swears he hates adulation yet drives around in a scarlet Rolls-Royce with the hood rolled down?'

Captain Smiley shrugged. 'He's given up 'spensive cars and champagne now, but for what? The quiet life here, which equals the square root of nuthin' far as I can see. You sure you not a friend of his?' he asked Keri again.

She shook her head. 'I took some photographs of him once, that's all.'

'How come Baz Guiler sprang to mind?' Shafe enquired, as the youth lolloped away.

'He didn't actually spring,' she confessed. 'Larry asked if I could look him up and see how the land lay with regard to someone from the *Enquirer* flying out to interview him. Others have tried before and got nowhere, so if he agreed it'd be quite a scoop.'

'Ha!' His laugh scraped like sandpaper. 'You have business in Barbados, too.'

'Hardly. I was to get in touch *only* if I had the time—as a favour.'

'But as it was Larry who asked the favour, you'll make time?'

'I might,' Keri prevaricated, feeling herself under siege.

'You've become——' Shafe twisted two fingers, one on top of the other '—like that with the personable Mr Roach again?'

'Larry sent a note after my father died and I telephoned to thank him, and—and I've called in at the offices on a couple of occasions,' she completed in a rush.

In fact, her visits to the newspaper headquarters had been more frequent, but she had no intention of providing details—not so long as Shafe remained in this unfamiliar mood. It was not a case of him simply being restless; his attitude towards her had something different about it. Something chary and intense. Something she did not trust.

'And now you intend to ask a favour of Baz Guiler?' he continued, as though she had never spoken.

'If he doesn't refuse to see me.'

'He won't. You know it, I know it and Larry Roach sure as hell knows it. Marvellous, isn't it? You take a set of photographs where some trick of the light conceals a guy's bald patch, and he's for ever grateful!'

'The photographs were a long time ago. Baz has probably forgotten about them, and about me. Besides, I haven't decided yet whether or not to approach him.'

'You will,' he said heavily. 'You will.'

Emma, thrusting small fists into her eyes as she awoke, provided a well timed diversion, for the vibes Shafe emitted were making Keri too anxious by half. In seconds the little girl's squirmings pierced Victor's sleep, and the two of them were blinking and stretching as Suzette called from the garden. Her offer to take charge allowed a release, and Shafe was only a yard behind Keri as she ran down the beach and plunged into the clear, surprisingly refreshing, water. A rope looped along a line of orange buoys marked off an area protected from the jet-skis and sail-boats which served the bay, so while Shafe swam back and forth in an energetic crawl, she dived down to inspect outcrops of coral.

The exercise made all the difference, and when Shafe emerged from the sea he was grinning. No further stabs were directed at Larry or the pop star, and for the remainder of the afternoon his attitude was easy. At dinner he brought her up to date on what her in-laws were doing, had her laughing at witty one-liners, remained safely low-key. Yet when Suzette and Victor departed everything tightened, as if by a spanner. The minutes goose-stepped tick-thump, tick-thump to seven-thirty, when Emma was tucked up in her cot. Sixty seconds later Shafe aggressively inspected his watch and his daughter scrambled up again.

'Dadda!' she called.

His reading of a fairy story did not close the toddler's eyes, but had the opposite effect of making her hyperactive. Keri could have prophesied as much, for the tale had been rushed, told in a voice spiked with ten thousand volts. How could anyone ignore his electric haste, let alone be lulled to rest?

'Maamee!' was the next summons, so while Shafe strode off to round up a rum punch, Keri sat in the bedroom rocking the child and singing songs, all to no avail.

It wasn't her fault if Emma would not go to sleep, she thought, her nerves growing frazzled. It wasn't her fault if Shafe's plans had been wrecked. Though they had not been wrecked, merely delayed. Why must he place so much emphasis—too much emphasis—on them making love at a specific time and to order? she wondered. Before, everything had happened naturally, spontaneously, effortlessly; now it was as though he needed to get her into bed in order to prove something—both to her and to himself. Keri gave a silent howl of protest. She hated this feeling of having his foot placed firmly on her neck, with no intention of release until it suited him.

Nine o'clock and her daughter's eyelids closing occurred simultaneously. Keri backed away from the cot, switched off the light and closed the door. A pause when she cocked an ear was rewarded with silence, then she swivelled. Her heart missed a beat. Shafe, crouched forward on the sofa with his drink clasped in two hands, reminded her of a sleek caged lion. His hair gleamed a tawny gold in the lamplight, an about-to-spring energy gripped his long legs, and the look when his eyes met hers warned of a lethal seriousness. Yet beneath it all, he seemed... bruised. Shafe bruised? Never. The command he had gained through years of dealing with many different people in many different countries ensured knocks were confidently and competently deflected. Though which knocks? Granted, winging around the world was not as happy-go-lucky as Angela insisted on making it sound, but he had full charge of a chosen life-style which he found endlessly satisfying. He was both free agent and a carefree one. Nothing and no one curtailed his activities—so far.

'Success,' she announced.

Dregs of punch were downed in a single swallow. 'Want one?' he asked, striding across to pour himself a refill.

Keri gave a giddy smile and said pointedly, *'After.'* She waited for a grin, a comic lift of an eyebrow, a rude remark, but Shafe did not react. She frowned. 'Are you OK?'

'No.'

A tiny word, yet it flooded the room.

'What's wrong?' she enquired, anxiety lifting her closer.

A long still moment crawled to eternity and back.

'I'm lonely,' he said, and his voice cracked. 'I've never felt as lonely in my whole life as I have over these past few weeks.'

'Lonely?' she repeated, her thoughts tangled and imprecise. He, the free agent, the dynamo who hurtled through time and continents on the count of three, the man who made a speciality of walking off into the sunset and leaving her behind, was complaining? How dared he! 'And I'm not?' she demanded.

'I guess in New York you could have been, but in London——' He slammed down his tumbler on a low table, the smack of glass against wood making her jump. 'Let's go to bed.'

Bed; the panacea, Shafe's remedy, his universal elixir. You want instant healing? Then hit the sack. Her spark of rebellion faltered. Perhaps he was right. Perhaps close physical contact was what they needed?

Keri repeated the giddy smile. 'I thought you'd never ask.' Even as the comment came out it jarred, sounded frivolous, maladroit. He disliked it as much as she, his distaste evident in the way he stiffened, in the hooding of his eyes. 'I mean——'

His mouth stopped her words in a kiss which tasted of rum and hunger, and his strong arms wound about her. Held close, Keri's heartbeat quickened. His hand came to her breast, but the restriction of the cotton top she wore annoyed him. He cursed, and cursed again on meeting the cream lace barrier of her bra. Roughly he pushed beneath it and she felt the heat of his hand against her skin. A fingertip scoured her nipple in a touch which was half-pleasure, half-pain. After being deprived for so long she ached for him to love her, but this need was too fierce, his actions too hasty. She must slow him down, soothe and calm and comfort. But he was hauling her into the bedroom, ripping open the buttons on his shirt with one hand while he held her with the other. A man in a fever, he flung the shirt aside and kissed her again, his mouth so hard that her lips were ground against her teeth. About to object, Keri heard the word said for her.

'No.' Shafe's hands fell away and he jolted back, as bemused as if he had collided with a wall. 'No,' he muttered, shaking his head.

'Not this way,' she agreed gently.

'Not at all.'

He had changed his mind? In a trice? At a whim? And after a day when he had conspired to build the sexual tension to crackling pitch?

'You don't want us to make love?' she queried, uneasily aware that he was looking at her as if she was someone he did not know, and did not want to know.

'Odd, isn't it? I thought I did, but now I—I can't go through with it.' His laugh was a bleak rasp. 'It's you.'

'Me?'

As rapidly as he had unfastened his shirt, he began to button it. 'You've stayed away too long. Far too long. When you gathered up Emma and flew over to see your father I had no idea you'd be deserting me for more than four damn months! It seems like a lifetime.'

Keri's stomach churned. She felt dispossessed, lost—and at fault. 'I never intended it to be for that long. I just . . . well, I couldn't leave Dad when he was so ill.'

'I don't begrudge the two months you spent with him one bit,' Shafe said impatiently, thrusting his shirt back into his trousers by the handful. 'What I can't understand is why you were still in London two months *after* the funeral.'

'I told you there were——'

'I know,' he rapped. 'Things to arrange.'

'Yes!' The prickle of guilty feelings thrust her on to the attack. 'Anyway, you were busy with various foreign assignments, so it's hardly been a case of you pining away in the solitary confinement of our apartment.'

'Perhaps if you'd been at the apartment, I'd have had a reason to try to be there.'

'And vice versa!' she shot back.

Shafe's grunt acknowledged the tit for tat. 'Sex isn't the answer to everything—or anything. Is it, Keri?' he appealed.

She had not been thinking of 'sex'; her image had been of loving limbs entwined, of fond intimacy, of the ultimate in communication between man and wife.

'I suppose not.'

'I reckon we should call it a day.'

'An early night?' she queried, at a loss to know what he meant.

'Yes. No. Yes.' He muttered an oath. 'You're reading me all wrong.' Folding his arms, Shafe began speaking in a stilted, lecturing kind of a way. 'We need time to talk our relationship out, and no distractions. No sex. Why I was so preoccupied with it, I've no idea. Will you sleep in Emma's room again, or would you prefer me to take a turn?'

Keri opened her mouth and promptly closed it. She felt pummelled, winded, squeegeed. His veto of them making love was bewildering enough, but to be told they were to sleep in separate rooms took all the life out of her. She struggled to make sense out of what was happening, the words he had said, the situation he had specified, but failed miserably. All that registered was the stark realisation that he did not want her near.

'You intend us to—to spend tonight apart?' she stammered at last.

He scowled. 'Tonight and maybe—oh, forget it. I don't want to talk about it now. You with Emma, or me?' he demanded.

'Er, me.'

CHAPTER THREE

FOR the second morning in Barbados Keri's fate was to awake alone, and late. Ten o'clock was a thread away, yet although she had gone to bed twelve hours earlier she had slept for a mere six. The remainder had been interminable wastelands of time, littered with painful brooding, conjectures and reviews. At the end of them all, nothing had been achieved.

When showering and dressing she made the usual noises—maybe left the bathroom door open to emphasise she was up and about?—but this time Shafe did not wander in. Surprise, surprise! His rejection and the haste with which he had said goodnight had been not only an insult to her sex appeal, but appeared to signify that rather than him sailing full steam ahead to strengthen their relationship, he could be harbouring doubts about its viability.

He was a traitor. Or had she been a fool? Could complaisantly granting him *carte blanche* to do his own thing have been not so much a sign of maturity as she had believed, but moronic carelessness? Expecting a good-looking male to go about his business without attracting the notice of the opposite sex now struck her as acutely naïve. Even Angela had once let it slip that she considered Shafe to be virile. He was. Her husband regarded the physical side of life as integral and inherently satisfying. In the months they had been apart there must have been temptations. Had he fought them successfully? Celibate he may have claimed to have been, but would he have boasted about an indiscretion? Keri flinched. An indiscretion? The idea was original and frightening, yet now it struck her, like a cold blade, that his talk of loneliness could be construed as a plea in mitigation. If sufficiently deprived, was he to be condemned for seeking comfort elsewhere?

Last night he had seemed as confused as she was about why he could not 'go through with it', but slot another woman into the background and didn't that explain everything? Torn between the two of them, wasn't it possible that making love had fixed itself in his mind as a much-needed clarification, the decisive factor? Shafe could have pinned his hopes on it showing him where his true affections lay. A man endowed with firm moral convictions, whose stated belief was that marriage should be 'for keeps', he would have yearned for his wife to win through. Keri felt decimated. It had not happened that way. Instead, mere *anticipation* had thrust him into retreat.

Disconsolately she threaded a narrow leather belt through the waist of her indigo jeans. Shafe's lack of desire had been as baffling and as agonising as if he had balled his fist and punched her between the eyes. She frowned. He had spoken of her 'reading him all wrong'; might she be in error again? Yet how else could she interpret last night's débâcle? Her fingers stilled as she recalled how he had always taken such deep delight in her body, and she in his. Physically their relationship had been solid gold. But how about the emotional side? Keri swallowed a draught of air, brutally acknowledging that ever since Emma's arrival there had been—not problems, that was too strong, yet it could not be denied that they had functioned better as a twosome than a three.

Why had Shafe said they needed to talk their relationship *out*? she wondered, sifting back piecemeal through the conversation. It could be regarded as just an expression—and occasionally his American phraseology did sit at odds with hers—yet on the other hand 'out' had a nasty ring of clearing the decks, getting things over and done with, finished. And what about 'I reckon we should call it a day'? Cold tremors brought goose-bumps. Admittedly of late their marriage had been one in name only, but he wasn't toying with the idea of—she gagged on the word—a divorce, was he? Her heart stopped dead, then started to thud erratically. Oh, God, please no, she begged in silent anguish. Divorce might happen to other people, but never to *them*.

Keri snapped the gilt clip on her buckle and straightened. Hold on. Simmer down. Get wise. She did not normally fall foul of rash imaginings, and to allow her thoughts to run rampant like this was fire-raising. The signals received last night had been mixed up, to say the least, and although in a split second Shafe may have performed a U-turn, it was only after an entire day of being obsessed with bulldozering her into bed. After a day when he had found it difficult to keep his hands off her. She thought of his kiss at the airport and his anger over her exit which had left them sleeping apart. Didn't such behaviour make it obvious that any tie with another woman—if there was another woman— must be flimsy? White teeth worried at a full lower lip. And, if added confirmation of the importance he invested in their marriage was needed, what about these six weeks? Would anyone, least of all a man in a hurry like Shafe, expend so much time on something they considered a doubtful, if not lost, cause? Never, she told herself. Like her, he had flown out to Barbados geared for a re-alignment which, *ipso facto*, meant survival. Last night had been a crazy hiccup, a lapse in his mental faculties, a nothing. Hadn't it? Yes, yes and yes. Head held high, she marched to the door. 'Happy ever after' remained as certain as ever.

Shafe was installed at the table, quack-quacking while he spooned a mixture of cornflakes and mashed banana into Emma's mouth. When she passed behind him the back of his tanned neck looked extremely kissable, but an inner apprehension kept her away.

''Morning,' Keri said in a sunny greeting and sat down beside the highchair. 'Shall I do that?' she offered, watching him scrape mush off his daughter's chin.

'No, thanks. Fathers like helping little girls, or didn't you know?'

Whump! she had been put in her place. Suzette, appearing from the kitchen with fresh supplies of coffee, demanded an exchange of greetings and forestalled any response. So that was the mood of the day, she thought as the housekeeper disappeared—muted aggression? But it took two to make a fight, and this morning her strategy was not to enter the ring, let alone act as sparring partner.

'You have no idea how nice it feels, having you around to take some of the strain,' Keri chirruped, as she squeezed lemon juice over a slice of orange papaya. 'Angela keeps her distance—she's always on pins in case Emma spills something over her or damages her tights—so I feel like I've been soldiering on alone for centuries.'

'Motherhood isn't unadulterated bliss? Strange, I had the impression it was totally absorbing. You know why Angela refuses to help, don't you?' Shafe continued, allowing no rebuttal. 'After a lifetime of lording it, to have her kid sister sneak out and win awards for photography, find herself a husband, albeit a damned Yank, then produce this angel child——' he chucked Emma under the chin '—is equivalent to being stabbed in the front. She'd rather die than admit it, but she's as envious as hell. Mind you, being a lazy bitch plays a part, too. I figure the aid she gave when your father was ill wouldn't have amounted to much?'

'It—it didn't,' Keri admitted, knocked askew by this unexpected condemnation.

Frustrating as her sister's lack of assistance had been, she had not complained—either to the offender or to Shafe. Angela did not take well to criticism, and there had been enough emotional strain to contend with, without her walking around in a huff. As far as not complaining to Shafe went, she regarded long-distance telephone moans as both a waste of costly minutes and tacky. Angela's faults might infuriate until her teeth clenched, but grousing about your own flesh and blood had always struck her as double-dealing.

'Ironical, isn't it?' he continued. 'Your father spends years cosseting her, while you're left to tag along. Yet——'

'She needed extra care,' Keri interjected. 'As a child, she spent six months in bed with scarlet fever and complications, and after that she was always going down with one bug or another.'

'I know, I know,' he said irritably. 'I also know that the whole household revolving around her has given her an inflated opinion of herself. How Angela can criticise right, left and centre, and never wonder if perhaps, just once, she might be wrong, beats me.'

'Maybe she has been spoilt, but after my mother dying you can understand why Dad was terrified something might happen to her, too. She did suffer from asthma attacks which——'

'Which, despite achieving the status of historical events, actually finished in her early teens, apart from the odd one which she manages to conjure up even now should a tight moment occur. I return to my point—that after the care and attention Angela received, she should have supported your father in his time of need. Instead, you're the one who rushes to help, while she discovers a sudden abhorrence of sickness. That performance of hers after the funeral made me want to throw up! "I couldn't bear to see Daddy so distressed",' he mimicked. 'Which, translated, meant, you carry on the good work, Keri, because I don't give a damn.'

'She did give a damn! Later she——'

'She what?' Shafe demanded, when Keri broke off. 'Shoot.'

How she wished she could. All she needed was a flesh wound, just enough of a graze to distract him. But she had said too much and painted herself into a corner where, in order to extricate herself, she must reveal frailties, something Angela would hate.

'Later, the way she'd avoided caring for Dad began to trouble her. She became agitated, miserable, wept all over the place. The doctor diagnosed depression.'

'You've kept very quiet about this.' He sounded angry.

Keri gave an awkward shrug. 'I didn't see the point in telling you, not when I could guess what your reaction would be. Dealing with your comments face to face would have been one thing, but long distance? No, thanks.'

'Maybe I wouldn't have oozed sympathy, but surely I'm not an ogre?' Shafe fed the last of the banana into an open rosebud of a mouth. 'Or maybe I am, at least over the telephone? I don't know why, but it does seem to bring out my worst. Doesn't make sense,' he reflected. 'Hell, stand me in front of a camera with a microphone and I'm at ease talking to millions. Yet stick a phone in my fist, position you at the other end of the line and I mess up. I hear myself becoming aggressive, saying things I don't quite mean.'

'I'm not much better,' Keri admitted, recalling how, over the past two months, their phone calls had deteriorated. 'I've often thought how when we're talking I sound like someone at a cocktail party, avidly discussing sweet nothing.'

He wiped Emma's mouth and her fingers. 'I guess Angela's fit of remorse would have demanded your unflagging attention?'

Keri nodded. 'The doctor asked me to keep an eye on her.'

'He believed she might be thinking along the lines of—of injuring herself?' Shafe faltered, in stunned surprise.

'No! It was simply a case of her feeling low and needing someone around to try and cheer her up.'

'I'm surprised she didn't stage a suicide attempt,' he remarked, showing no compunction about mocking, now it was clear there had been no danger. Doubtless, his sister-in-law was not as bad as he made her out to be, but her bred-in-the-bone habit of using people made it difficult to give her his sympathy. Simply feeling low or not, he had no doubt she would have been laying on the agony. 'Can't you imagine the scene—a silken-robed Angela draped fetchingly over the sofa, an empty bottle of pills in one hand, a tear-stained farewell note in the other. It would appeal to her sense of theatre.'

'You are the most cynical man I know,' Keri flashed.

'You ought to get around more. Still, at last you've provided me with one proper reason for why you delayed coming home.'

She threw him a look, but he had risen to lift Emma from the highchair and his head was averted. One proper reason? Shafe implied that her talk of how she had needed to meet with lawyers, insurance men and the bank manager in order to sort out her father's affairs had been so much candyfloss. In addition, he seemed to imply there were other, equally significant reasons why she had not instantly returned to New York—and to him. Of course, there were, but...

Keri finished her coffee, pushed back her chair. This start to the day suggested a succession of broadsides being fired off, but she was damned if she would lie beside him on the beach and provide a ready target. Better to keep moving.

'Suppose we try and find Baz Guiler this morning?' she suggested, in a tone rippling with 'wouldn't it be fun?'

His lip curled. 'Visit the sore with the bare head?'

'If you're not interested, I'm happy to take the moke.'

'Not possible until you've fixed a local driver's permit,' he said, breaking off from a resumption of the duck noises which had Emma fascinated. 'But do you think I'd let you, the woman who zips away from traffic lights at Mach Two while cab drivers gaze on in admiration, loose in a moke with my daughter strapped in the back?' He placed his cheek against the soft pink cheek of the child in his arms. 'No way.'

'I might drive fast, but I don't drive danger-ously,' Keri protested. 'However, I wasn't in-tending to take your daughter. I thought we could ask Suzette if she'd look after her.'

'Leave her here?'

Shafe sounded astonished, though whether it was with the idea or rather that it came from her, she could not tell. He also sounded reluctant.

'Why not? Granted, it puts Victor at risk of more grievous bodily harm, but so long as we sneak out without alerting Emma she'll be fine. A girl I know in London runs a tiny tots' playgroup, a casual affair in her own home, and I've taken Emma along occasionally,' Keri explained. 'She yelled for the first five minutes when I saw her down with the other kids and disappeared, but after that she loved it. Being stuck in a house day after day with adults was bad for her. She had no other children to play with, no stimulation, no outlet for her energy.' Wondering whether now might be the time to admit to her major motive in dispatching the toddler, she threw Shafe a look, but the jut of his jaw warned against confessions. 'Emma's a sociable little girl,' she finished up. 'She enjoys company.'

'A playgroup sounds an excellent idea.'

Being awarded his approval felt outrageously good, and Keri grinned.

'Wouldn't coming with me to see Baz Guiler be a good idea?' she suggested. 'Maybe this programme about Joey will be the only profile you ever do, but who knows? If you made contact with Baz——'

'The last thing I need right now is contact with a guy who's a mass of self-inflicted love-bites,' Shafe interrupted irreverently.

'But surely it'd be to your advantage to meet him? Don't forget he is the writer of some incredibly sensitive songs, and he is newsworthy, on both sides of the Atlantic. Even though he's been out of the limelight for a couple of years, he hasn't been forgotten. His records continue to sell by the hundreds of thousands, if not millions. Likewise posters. Bedroom walls all over the Western world bear his likeness.'

Shafe remained unimpressed. 'Shows how effective publicity hype can be. Apart from the music, what've you got? A balding, middle-aged man with a habit of spouting the most insincere drivel you've ever heard.'

'Maybe, yet walk into a crowded room and mention his name, and I guarantee most of the women present'll go woozy.'

'They might, I wouldn't. I don't care for the guy, and once he recognised my apathy chances are it'd bring on one of those legendary tantrums of his.

That wouldn't help your cause, would it? Or should I say friend Larry's?'

'You've never met him, so you don't know whether you'd like him or not,' Keri said, wishing he would not sound so antagonistic whenever he referred to the newspaperman. 'Though,' she had to concede, 'what you say about him is true.'

'But?'

She had forgotten how well Shafe knew her. How he could read her silences as well as her speech.

'I was only in Baz's company briefly and he was obnoxious for the most part, but somehow it was as though he provided the sulks, the demands, the outsized ego, because he saw them as textbook requirements for the temperamental pop idol.'

'Guiler's a victim of his own myths?'

She nodded. 'It struck me that beneath it all he could be . . . vulnerable.'

'So spake the soft-hearted Keri. The guy's as vulnerable as pig iron!' Emma had been growing restless, eager to join Victor who had been peeking at her from around the kitchen door, so he set her down on her feet and tapped her bottom. 'Off you go, smarty pants. Wonder if she'll have a pert little rump like yours when she grows up?' Shafe mused, as the toddler scampered off. He stuck his hands in the hip pockets of his Levis, and frowned. 'About last night. It's high time I explained that——'

At his intensity, Keri froze. Earlier she had passed off his rejection as of little consequence—almost— but now confessed to deceiving herself. In reality it represented a nebulous area, one with which she had yet to come to terms. She could raise no enthusiasm for him explaining, possibly about another woman, not seconds after he had praised her backside!

'It wasn't important,' she said at speed.

'It sure as hell was important to *me*. I never ever imagined I'd—we'd—reach the stage where——'

'Let's leave it.'

'Leave it!' Shafe gave a strangled laugh. 'May I take a second here to remind you that——'

'For now,' she pleaded, desperate to escape being reminded of anything. She recognised her ignorance as the makeshift and temporary raft it was, but needed it to carry her over the marriage rapids, at least for today. Maybe by tomorrow she would feel more able to cope with a ducking—or was she destined to be drowned? 'As you didn't want to become involved in discussions yesterday, so I'd prefer us to take time off now. Can't we simply soak up the sunshine and track down Baz Guiler? Please.'

For a long moment he looked at her, then he sighed and agreed with her request.

The map left much to be desired, and it took two false starts before Keri managed to navigate them on to an undulating road which cut inland across the island towards St Philips. Skirting sugar cane plantations and acres planted with groundnut, the route led them through tranquil West Indian villages where schoolboys stopped playing cricket to wave. The pace was slow and easy. Driving along in the sunshine was fun. A conversation with a verge-cutter who ceased his chores, rested his machete on his shoulder, and explained the local geography at length, corrected a wrong turn at a crossroads, and in time they arrived at Ginger Bay.

In contrast to the tranquil wooded bays of the
Platinum Coast, the terrain here was wilder and
open. White-topped breakers which had gathered
strength on their journey across the Atlantic
pounded at the base of craggy cliffs, dampening
the air with spray. Tourists did venture this far—
Keri had noticed several quaint restaurants and a
pink-washed hotel tucked among the by-roads—but
not so many. The area was less travelled, much
quieter, and accurately suited the cliché of 'off the
beaten track'. In choosing to make his home here,
Baz Guiler had chosen well. Indeed, as someone
who had, for almost two decades, kept the phrase-
makers of Grub Street busy reporting his raucous
life-style, high profile attendance at night-clubs,
ferociously leaked love affairs, the hardened at-
tention-seeker had exhibited consummate skill in
becoming a recluse.

'The second turn, according to Captain Smiley,'
Keri said, inching her finger along the thin red line,
but none of the turns looked more than cart tracks,
and signposts had become a thing of the past.

'Don't do this to me, Basil,' Shafe muttered as,
having decided they had gone too far, he swept back
along the same stretch of road for a third time.

'Want to pack it in?'

'And disappoint your dear friend Larry? Good
God, no. There's an opening here, let's give it a
try.'

Sweeping in through ancient stone gateposts, he
steered them down a narrow rutted lane. Overhung
by shaggy bearded banyan trees which allowed only
occasional rays of sunshine to penetrate, the light
was dim and when, fifty yards on, they emerged
into the open, the glare dazzled. Keri raised a hand

to her eyes. The lane had tapered off into nothing, leaving them at the edge of a raggedy oval of long grass. Bushes of pink-orange bougainvillaea cascaded in crescents on both sides, while directly ahead stood a small bungalow, half hidden behind an overgrown hedge. Unprepossessing, with bleached white walls and a burnt clay tiled roof, it shimmered in the haze of morning heat. As Shafe turned off the ignition, engine noise was replaced by the sound of calypso coming from someone's stereo.

'Found him!' Keri exclaimed.

'It isn't just rock stars who take their decibels mega-loud,' Shafe pointed out, grimacing against the beat which filled the air, thrummed in their ears, required them to speak with raised voices.

'The music doesn't matter, the clue is the name of the house.' She gestured towards a black wrought iron sign fixed to one side of the porch. '*Jocasta,*' she read. 'Remember Jocasta Sinclair?'

'The teenaged temptress he lived with for a while? But he tossed her on to the scrap heap the same as all his other women, so why would he name the place after her?'

'No idea. Bet I'm right, though.'

'Go and enquire.' Shafe tapped a percussion on the steering wheel. 'If Guiler does hang out here and he's willing to enter into discussions, suppose I come back in, say, an hour?'

The discovery that she was to be dropped off had Keri frowning. Admittedly, broaching the subject of an interview with a volatile character like Baz Guiler was something to be done unhurriedly and with care, but she had taken it for granted Shafe would wait. She felt a sudden chill. Of late, she seemed to be taking far too much for granted where he was concerned.

'Where will you go in the meantime?' she demanded.

'I intend to drive into Bridgetown and make contact with the management of the *Bajan Buccaneer*,' Shafe informed her smoothly. 'Arrangements have been made over the phone, but I need to confirm them. And, as you're attending to your business affairs, this would seem the ideal opportunity for me to attend to mine.' Alert to her chagrin, he grinned. 'I trust you're not thinking about putting me in a headlock?'

Keri's chin lifted. 'Would I?'

He lolled back in his seat and surveyed her through steady grey eyes.

'You might try.'

She climbed out of the moke, tugged at the pointed collar of her cyclamen-coloured shirt and stepped towards the house.

'If Guiler is in residence, make sure you keep your knees together,' Shafe called behind her, but she ignored him.

To the increasing thump of music, Keri walked up between rows of stiff Norfolk pines and rampaging frangipani to a glass-panelled front door. She jammed her finger on the bell and waited. No reply. Not so amazing, considering that a klaxon call would sink without trace among the cacophony of drums and guitars. Head held high, and resolutely not looking back at the man monitoring her progress, she marched around to the corner of the building. Like the front, the garden to the rear was a tropical jungle, seemingly untouched by human hand for years. Pausing midway to untangle a branch which caught in her hair, she went along an overgrown path to the edge of a covered patio. By now the music had reached bedlam level and she identified a stereo unit, its cable snaking back into the bungalow, as the source. Her gaze lengthened. Beyond the stereo, half in sun, half in shade, a sunbed had been positioned and a man in baggy navy shorts lay face down across it. His feet were bare and—her mouth twitched—so was the top of his head. The immaculate positioning and lacquering of his hair had ensured Baz Guiler's baldness remained one of show business's best kept secrets, but today a pink-brown scalp shone like a beacon through dishevelled dark strands. Was he asleep or merely resting? Whatever, rag-doll limbs indicated he had gone splat.

Keri cleared her throat, coughed, and said 'Excuse me' a couple of times, but her voice, like the doorbell, did not stand a chance. Either she bellowed in his ear or disposed with the opposition. She chose the latter, and as she lifted the needle from the record blessed peace descended. There was a moment when a bee droned, when a snatch of birdsong sounded, then Baz Guiler came to life.

'Who the so-and-so are you?' he demanded, peering blearily back over his shoulder.

In slow motion he rolled over and fumbled into a sitting position. Yawning and dragging his hands down stubbled cheeks, Keri was relieved to see he looked more curious than annoyed. Perhaps life on an island in the sun had calmed his notorious temper? Or maybe he had yet to come properly awake?

'I'm Keri Rokeby, used to be Napier. I worked for Larry Roach on the *Enquirer* and I once took

some photographs of you. Back in England,' she
added, as his gaze slid past her. Judging by the difficulty he was experiencing in focusing his eyes, he
must have been deep asleep. 'When Larry knew I
was coming out here on holiday, he asked me to
look you up. I have a ——' she cleared her throat
'—a request, and I'd be grateful if you could spare
me some time to talk about it.'

A tattooed arm waved expansively. 'Take as much
time as you want, flower.'

'Thanks,' she grinned, barely able to believe her
luck. 'My husband's waiting outside, so I'll go and
tell him to collect me later.'

The arm waved again. 'Bring him in. The more
the merrier.'

'He has some business to attend to in
Bridgetown.'

'Fine. Fine.'

Deciding that even if this reception was too good
to be true she would be a fool not to take advantage, Keri rushed out and dispatched Shafe, who
left with what she felt was indecent haste and enthusiasm. It was only when the rumble of the moke
had faded and she was walking back that reasons
for Baz Guiler's unusual amiability suddenly hit.
Could he be drunk, or maybe high on drugs? Rec-
ollections of the rock 'n' roll milieu he had fre-
quented said either or both were possible.
Chastising herself for a shortage of basic intelli-
gence, Keri perched on the chair he indicated. The
instruction to keep her knees together no longer
seemed droll, it made sense. Past media gossip had
classified Baz Guiler as a seducer *extraordinaire*.
Too full of his own importance to equably accept

a refusal, what did she do if he suddenly decided to lunge?

'Are you enjoying life in Barbados?' she enquired, the question masking a rapid search for signs of what his affliction might be.

'Love it. Great to escape the hullabaloo. All the publicity was driving me mad.'

Though Keri would have readjusted the words and said he had been mad for publicity, she produced a dutifully sympathetic smile.

'Hand on heart——' a palm slapped the gold medallion which lay against his hairy chest '——being so many people's god was a heavy responsibility. Any concerned member of the human race would have felt the same. Found fame by accident,' he harrumphed. 'Never sought it. Had it thrust upon me. Though I know why I was chosen. I have an in-built affinity with rhythm and——' he hiccuped '——I hope this doesn't sound conceited, but when I perform on stage there's this aura which I rarely see in others.' He held out his arms as if expecting to receive fulsome bouquets of agreement. 'Star quality.'

The maudlin assertions and hiccups suggested Baz Guiler could be drunk, a fact confirmed when her nostrils were assailed by the waft of what appeared to be one hundred per cent proof whisky. Drunk, and overjoyed that the gods had seen fit to deliver an audience.

'Everyone thinks I'm a toughie, but don't you believe it.' He staggered to his feet. 'I'll get you a drink, flower. What'll it be?'

'Orange, please,' Keri replied, deciding the best way—indeed, the only way—to tackle the situation was to humour him.

He disappeared inside the bungalow and was gone for ages. She heard a distant crash, a muttering, but ultimately he emerged, weaving his way towards her with a glass in each hand. She received juice as specified, while he wandered back to the lounger, clutching his whisky and water as though it was a family heirloom.

In silence, her host gulped down half the glass. In silence, she surveyed him. Despite the receding hairline and lines around his eyes which put him in his forties, Baz Guiler sober could be said to evoke the green-eyed black-haired appeal of a faded pirate. Drunk, however, he evoked nothing more than Shafe's description: a balding, middle-aged man who, since she had last seen him, had added several pounds in weight, most of which dwelt around his middle.

'Inside me there's a yard-wide streak of soft centre,' he declared, whisky splashing on to the flagstones as he made another grandiloquent gesture. He sucked dribbles from his fingers. 'You ask my mother, and any others who have known me.'

This avowal proved to be the starting-off point for a marathon monologue on what a fun guy he was. Commencing with his schooldays, he ponderously took her through to when he had hit the big time, and then on. Murmuring appropriate noises, Keri drank her juice and wondered how best to steer him back to the purpose of her visit. But interrupting an inflated ego was not easy, and the tropical heat imparted a feeling of inertia.

'Wanna take my picture again?' Baz enquired, in the midst of droning on about the smash hits he had written. 'Y'know, Jo liked those pictures you did. I had a few put into a white leather album and she carried it around with her wherever she went. Jo loved that little album.' Suddenly he stopped talking, bowed his head and clamped a thumb and forefinger to the bridge of his nose to stem the flow of tears. 'Once Jocasta loved me.'

Keri stared at him in alarm. His mouth was quivering, his face contorted with pain. An outburst of bad temper she had anticipated, maybe a stab at seduction, but never him breaking down.

'Please. Don't,' she appealed.

'Without Jo, my life is empty. I've tried to fill the gap with other women, but it doesn't work. I came out here hoping a different environment might help, but it hasn't.' He swallowed hard, his Adam's apple rising and falling. 'I loved her so much. I still do. We never should have split, but—but I couldn't treat her as she needed to be treated, and she left.'

'I understood you left her?' Keri suggested tentatively.

'Nah, that was just the story my agent put about. Couldn't have a famous sex-symbol like Baz Guiler being jilted, could we?' he gibed bitterly. 'But Jo was the one who wanted out. It was all my fault. I let her down. I tried to make it happen, to——' He ran out of words. 'I failed her,' he muttered, rallying. 'I couldn't——' The word supply failed again and there was a fraught pause until once more he rallied. 'She was fifteen years younger than me. Well, nearer twenty. That was the trouble. I was too old for her. Couldn't cope. I guess the generation gap got in the way and made us incompatible. Don't quote me on that,' he said sharply, as a ray of sensibility pierced his haze.

'I won't,' Keri assured him. 'I'm not a reporter.'

'Nah, nah.' Reporter or not, his visitor had something to do with the Press, and in-built experience belatedly advised against talking too freely. 'You said you and your husband were here on holiday,' he mumbled, in a ham-fisted attempt to turn the tables. 'Where are you staying?'

'We have a bungalow on the Platinum Coast.'

'Just the two of you, is it?'

'No, our little girl's with us.'

'Never had a family myself, though there's still time. How old is your daughter?'

'Fifteen months.'

'Beginning to get up to all the tricks at that age.'

She smiled. 'Yes. If I let her loose in a supermarket, it's murder! She can't pass anything without making a grab.'

'Like at the bottom one in a pyramid of cans?'

Keri laughed. 'How did you guess? That happened last week, in the one second when I had my back turned. It was a delayed crash, so Emma had managed to move out of the way before everything collapsed but, oh dear, the embarrassment.'

She did not know how it had happened, yet all of a sudden they had swapped roles and she was the one doing the talking. The odd thing was, Baz Guiler listened with keen interest, appearing to find the tales of Emma as fascinating as she did.

'You should have seen her in the sea yesterday,' Keri said, arriving at the latest anecdote.

'I wish I had.'

His note of sincerity was beguiling, and before she could stop herself the incident had been described and she had even added the suggestion that he might like to visit them one day. It was only after their address had been supplied that she returned to her senses. What a dummy! This man had spent years in the fast lane. He was hard-boiled, brittle, even decadent. He had seen everything, been everywhere, done everything. Inviting him to watch her infant daughter at play was inane. Only the excessive consumption of alcohol must have stopped him from laughing in her face.

'The—er—request I mentioned,' she said, returning to the reason for her visit. 'Larry—that's Larry Roach of the *Enquirer*,' she reminded him, 'asked me to ask if you'd be agreeable to being interviewed. He's thinking in terms of an in-depth series of articles which would appear over four or five days. Something on the lines of one man and his music. How you started, what the influences were, how you keep the creative juices flowing.'

Baz raised a hand to adjust errant strands of hair. 'Not interested.'

'Couldn't you think it over?' Keri appealed.

'No.' He clambered to his feet. 'Fancy another drink?'

'Not for me.' Because they had been getting along so well together the abruptness of his refusal jolted. It also served to thrust her into candour, and she added, 'I don't think you should have another one, either. Being under the influence at——' Keri inspected her wristwatch and discovered, to her dismay, that she had been in his company for almost an hour and a half '—noon, can't be good for you.'

His backbone became a ramrod. 'If you're suggesting I'm an alcoholic, I bloody am not!'

'You were sober this time yesterday?'

Baz Guiler glared. 'I object to that question.'

'Were you?' Some obstinate quirk made her persist.

'Who the hell are you to burst in here and start putting me on the rack?'

'I'm not. All I'm asking is——' Her candour fizzled out. What *was* she asking? What was she doing? Keri gulped in a breath. To so much as hint at an idea as emotive as him drinking to excess had been madness. His rages were notorious. Why hadn't she remembered them? 'Um, haven't you had enough? You're a gifted musician who regularly received gold discs, platinum discs for your work,' she waffled, 'and——'

'Now I'm a burnt-out case, is that it?' he growled.

'Not at all.'

'You think I haven't been composing while I've been in Barbados?'

'I'm sure you have,' Keri replied swiftly, though she would have bet money his days were devoted to the steady intake of alcohol. 'Thank you for sparing me your time. If you change your mind about speaking to someone from the *Enquirer*, you know where to get in touch.'

'I shan't.' After a wary inspection of the hand she had extended, Baz risked a brief shake. 'Enjoy the rest of your holiday,' he mumbled and, ostentatiously taking hold of his glass, headed for the house.

Through the garden she went, and down the path out on to the grassy oval.

'Sorry I'm late,' she said, rushing up to the moke. 'The time just seemed to fly past.'

'No sweat. I've only been back five minutes myself. I was worrying about *you* having to hang around. Well, how did it go?' Shafe asked, as she climbed in beside him.

'It didn't, so far as Baz agreeing to an interview is concerned. Yet, despite him becoming aggressive and being drunk——'

There was a low whistle. 'At this time of the day?'

'Thoroughly pickled. Yet, despite that, plus him boasting and generally being a pain, I still had the feeling that, given the chance to know him better, you could find he grows on you.'

'Like fungus.' Shafe slid into gear and they set off towards the lane. 'So—what happened?'

'We talked, or rather Rent-a-mouth talked. He started off by singing a lengthy requiem in praise of the glorious me. However, later he spoke about his affair with Jocasta Sinclair. It appears the difference in age made them incompatible.'

'Incompatible? That's a well used but very vague term. What did he mean?'

Keri explained by quoting the rock star's words as accurately as she could.

'He reckoned the twenty-year age difference left him unable to cope,' she finished up.

'The guy was impotent?' Shafe suggested.

Her peal of laughter dismissed such a hopelessly bizarre idea. 'Nuts! He's a grand master where the opposite sex is concerned. In his time, he's reputed to have made the earth move for half the actresses and beauty queens in the Western world.'

'So?'

'He's not that decrepit,' she chided. 'Maybe age has nothing to do with it, but——'

'Nothing,' he intoned, in a clipped voice.

'All Baz meant was that he and the girl had problems relating on a day-to-day basis.'

'Impotent.'

'Never!' Keri scoffed.

'How can you be sure?'

'I can't, but——'

'It's a common condition which can happen to anyone at any time.'

'Not to a man like Baz,' she asserted. 'He's much too confident.'

'If you think it's only nervous wrecks who suffer that way, you're wrong.'

A hoarseness in his tone drew her eyes to his profile and, in particular, to the grim slant of his jaw. There was a moment of silence when she wallowed in confusion, in vague ideas, in stumbling half-thoughts, then Keri took a mental leap. She could not imagine any reason why Shafe should voice such an unusual concept, unless...

Her mind travelled back—to the previous night.

CHAPTER FOUR

'Do you intend to try again?'

'What?' Keri asked, startled.

If a grenade had exploded at her feet, she could not have been more completely thrown. Bring the inadequacy she had laughingly derided mere seconds ago into closer focus, and it became unbearably tragic. Sympathy welled up inside her. Poor Shafe. Poor darling Shafe. If that's what had occurred yesterday, how devastated he must have been, must still be feeling. How churned-up, how stricken, how flawed.

'The last thing you'll want is to go back to Larry empty-handed,' he said, using a combative monotone, 'so I wondered whether you were planning to visit Guiler a second time?'

'No.'

She warned herself against jumping to conclusions. Looked at realistically, the idea of a gung-ho male like her husband working himself up into such a state of nervous tension that he had been rendered incapable had to be far-fetched. And yet a part of Keri asked, why not?

'Just no?'

'I told Larry I'd do my best and I have. Win some, lose some,' she replied, as a sly voice insisted the only reason she was giving the notion any weight at all could be laid at the door of sheer desperation. Didn't she need an excuse to banish the 'other woman'? And wouldn't she sooner believe Shafe

77

had rejected her because he'd been unable to make love, rather than because he preferred to make love to someone else?

'You're giving up easily. Doesn't Larry de- serve——'

'Why this obsession with Larry?' she demanded, tempted now to burst into gales of manic laughter. Not only was Shafe free of the least hang-up where sex was concerned, he was entirely laid back. And she must be having a brainstorm.

'*I'm* not obsessed with the guy,' he retorted.

'Neither am I!'

Whatever Shafe's physical condition, his mental state showed signs of testiness. Once, the light-hearted affinity she and the bespectacled features editor had shared had amused him; now, for some reason, it rankled. Though, of course, Keri re-alised, as her thoughts performed another loop-the-loop and this time slumped into desolation, if Shafe was in the process of transferring his affections, most things about her *would* rankle. What had charmed would now irritate. What had attracted would become repellent. Her blue eyes grew misty. Hadn't he been repelled last night?

'It was the devil's own job tracking down the *Bajan Buccaneer*'s offices,' he commented. 'There were signs pasted up all over the harbour area, but they took you round in circles. When I did strike base, the guy I wanted to see had disappeared for an early lunch and no one else was interested. Mention USB News and the usual reaction is for folk to leap to their feet and salute. Everyone wants to be on television. Everyone except this crowd. They had other priorities, like yakking on about a fishing trip or enjoying a quiet smoke.'

'Oh.'

'Just oh?' he queried.

He had grinned, and Keri fastened frenziedly on to this as a sign that whatever it was which underscored their problems, it was something which could be solved. If another woman had wandered into his life, she would make sure the intruder damn well wandered out again. Or if Shafe had been emasculated last night—well, that could be dealt with, too. Arbitrarily dismissing her see-sawing thoughts, she turned her attention to his morning.

'So, did you manage to confirm the arrangements?'

'Eventually.'

His account of people having 'gone walkin' 'bout' and the 'gone walkin' 'bout' of any record of previous telephone conversations with the network was involved and amusing. His tale finished as they drove up to the bungalow, but then any chance Keri might have had of unscrambling the truth of what had happened the previous night faded as a smiling Emma tottered up to greet them.

'Look, look!' the toddler urged, taking hold of their hands and dragging them round to the patio to exclaim over a piece of paper bearing crayon strokes drawn in their absence.

'Did she miss us?' Shafe asked Suzette.

'Once, but I produced a lollipop and that did the trick.'

'Callous young miss,' he scolded, cuddling the culprit.

Lunch arrived hotfoot, followed by a second afternoon on the beach. In addition to Victor joining in the fun, this time they were adopted by a couple of older boys. Pot Boo and Sharkey—they

insisted those were their given names—were eight
and ten respectively and, although they appeared
to be playing truant from school, they were keen
to learn all they could about the States and England.
There were non-stop questions, a ball game and
swimming. Another visit from Captain Smiley—
who neglected to mention his jewellery, despite a
twenty-minute stay—was terminated when Emma's
eyelids showed signs of drooping. Bathtime provoked a temporary revival, but it was all Keri could
do to keep her awake to eat dinner. Bedtime was
prompt and sleep instant.

If only her daughter had been so obliging the
previous evening, she thought wistfully as she
walked out on to the patio where Shafe was reading.
Then, perhaps, her husband would not have drunk
so much rum punch, then perhaps he would not
have become so keyed up, then perhaps he would
have swept her into his arms and carried her off to
bed—and to ecstasy. Or would he? Keri sank down
into a chair and gazed blindly out into the darkness
of the tropical night.

Shafe turned a page and looked up. 'Why the
faraway expression?'

A bubble of frantic laughter threatened to escape.
How did she reply... It's because I'm puzzled. You
see, although I know you were aroused when you
lay on the bed with me yesterday morning, I'm un-
decided about your reaction at night. To be frank,
I suspect there might not have been a reaction.
Please could you set me straight...?

But how could she raise doubts about his
prowess? There were, she remembered reading, two
things a man will never admit he can't do well—
drive and make love, and as issues went the loss of

manhood soared sky-high on the sensitivity scale. Of crucial importance to any male, let alone one as inherently vital and red-blooded as Shafe, it would have struck at the core of his image of himself as masculine. Demanding he admit to such a deficiency was something she could not do. If he told her, it must be of his own free will. But then, of course, maybe he would regard the subject as equivalent to a state secret and not be able to bring himself to speak of it, ever. Alternatively—her mouth went dry—maybe if she *did* ask the question he would give a belly laugh and inform her that although she didn't appeal, he was currently enjoying a rabbity sex life with some mistress or other.

'I—I was thinking how noisy the night is in the Caribbean. Tweets and windbell sounds seem to start up at dusk and go all the way through until dawn.'

To Keri the reply sounded contrived, but he appeared to accept it, and as he returned to his book she returned to her thoughts. The time when she could have questioned Shafe about such a sensitive issue *had* existed. Once, there had been no forbidden areas between them, no holding back, but now... She sighed. Now, although they talked, they seemed to say very little. Why had everything changed? What had brought about this deterioration in their relationship? Back in London she would have heaped all the blame on his career and the way it separated them, yet with Shafe close by in the lamplight this took on an air of the glib, righteous kind of answer her sister would produce.

Keri nibbled at a fingernail. How could she discover the reason why he had changed his mind last

night without voicing an actual question? The obvious solution was to entice Shafe into bed, but . . .
As in any man/woman relationship, there had been occasions when she had flirted, teased, aroused him by playing the wanton both on a conscious and subconscious level, yet to seduce him in cold blood seemed entirely different. It smacked of the gruesomely comic. And suppose Shafe failed to respond, what then? How did she interpret his lack of interest—as a sign she no longer possessed the power to excite him, or rather that he could not be excited? He *would* respond, she assured herself. He must.

It was ironical how their roles had switched. Yesterday Shafe had been the one doggedly determined to get them horizontal, now it was her turn. She sneaked him a glance. Sprawled in the chair, with his legs stretched out and his Levis stretched tight across his hips, he was a most attractive man. Loose-limbed and lean, he moved with an innate elegance. She liked the way he walked, she liked the way he looked, and even if the moustache continued to seem strange she had to admit she liked the cavalier charm it bestowed. Keri ran her tongue over her lips. Should she disappear into the bedroom, don her black lace, thigh-slitted nightdress, spray on perfume, request his presence and wait? Speculation made her tingle deep inside, then she frowned. Such a glaring come-on could prove counterproductive. Subtlety must be the name of the game.

'Care for something to drink?' she enquired with studied diffidence, thinking that drinks would enable her to move her chair up to his, place a table before them and—allow her arm to casually drape itself around his shoulder?

'Not right now.' Shafe closed his book with a decisive snap. 'I know we agreed discussions were a no-go area today, but you're obviously chewing things over and I've also been doing some thinking.' Dark-gold strands were pushed clear of his brow. 'What you said yesterday about making a legit-imate observation rather than blowing off steam has been troubling me. I gained the impression "observation" equated with "grievance", which makes me think you could have come to Barbados all set to embark on a crusade.'

'A crusade?' Keri echoed, dismayed to find the man she was intending to seduce had become stern-jawed and earnest all of a sudden.

'Yup. The occasions when you march with a banner don't occur too often—thank God, because when they do you march to the bitter end—but at such times you get a fanatical glint in your eyes. I've noticed that glint today.'

March to the bitter end? Fanatical glint? She ob-jected to his choice of words. He seemed to be de-picting an infatuation with an ill-conceived idea, when it was not like that at all. Keri would admit to being dedicated—was it a sin?—but her plans were not rash or rushed. Indeed, the hours she had spent structuring them in London must total hundreds.

'And what kind of a crusade am I supposed to have in mind?' she replied, as airily as she could.

'Something like insisting I comply with X, Y and Z parameters, or else——' He drew a finger across his tanned throat. 'Sorry, I'm not the kind of animal who can submit to a nine-to-five existence.'

Instantly Keri felt queasy. 'You mean, you'd turn down the position of newscaster if you were approached a second time?' she demanded, her breathlessness betraying her horror. 'Yes, I'm aware the network offered it to you before,' she added, when his jaw hardened.

'How? Who told you?'

'Someone rang in your absence and happened to mention it.' She leafed back through time. 'It was Mr Spiro.'

'So the big boss spilled the beans. Why didn't you say you knew?' Shafe demanded.

'Why didn't you say the position had been handed to you on a plate?' Keri retaliated. 'Bill Spiro didn't spell it out in exact words, but it was clear he thought you were mad to refuse, and so did I! As a newscaster you'd have an excellent salary, status, a——'

'Don't talk about the damn job as though it's sacrosanct,' he muttered. 'All newscasting means is that I'd be doomed to spend the rest of my life reading words off a goddamn autocue. It's Mickey Mouse stuff.'

'It can't be so bad that coming home each night wouldn't compensate,' she appealed.

'Honey, I hate to rain on your parade,but——'

'Bill Spiro gave me to understand that if you felt like taking up the job at a later date it'd be open to you,' Keri said eagerly. 'If you were a newscaster we wouldn't need to live so near the airport. Instead we could buy a——'

Shafe heaved a sigh. 'Look, you knew what the deal was when you married me, and up until now you've accepted my absences. I can even remember you saying how they added a spice, a flavour, a joy

to the times when we *were* together. And they did,
Keri, they did. They do,' he adjusted, after an im-
perceptible pause. 'There's always been a magic between you and me.'

She gave a bleak laugh. There was no magic now,
just a hard nub of despair rattling around inside
her like a pebble in an empty drum.

'You——' she swallowed '—you aren't prepared
to settle down.'

'I'm not prepared to be *nailed* down!'

A taut, gripping silence fell between them with
an almost audible thud. How could he dismiss her
plans, those plans she had constructed with such
care and attention? Keri wondered, feeling bereft.
How could he flick them aside, like so much trash?
How could he *waste* them? Once, she had regarded
a shared life with Shafe as the culmination of all
her dreams; now, the future resembled a nightmare.
He might have wanted to sit and talk, but whatever
subject he had had in mind it had been light years
away from what Coleridge, the poet, termed 'creative self-modification'! So why had Shafe suggested they meet up in Barbados? She did not
understand. Neither did she understand how he
could give newscasting the go-by. Keri wanted to
rage against his contrariness, beat her fists against
his chest, shout out against the injustice.

'Humph!'

The exclamation contained all the reproach she
could muster.

'We should be discussing a lot more than me rejecting a newscaster's job,' Shafe remarked.

What he meant, she supposed, was that they
should be discussing what had happened last night.
Last night did not matter! After rejecting her blue-

print for their future, did he imagine she cared about his rejection of *her*! Maybe she should but, rightly or wrongly, she found it impossible to become involved now. Not now when her heart was breaking.

Keri rose to her feet. 'I'm going to bed,' she announced.

'But, toots, it isn't even nine o'clock.'

'I'm tired,' she said, stiffly aware of the endearment.

'Toots', uttered in Shafe's husky way, brought all kinds of memories to mind. It was a derivative of 'tootsie-wootsie', a term he had first delivered with a broad grin in the knowledge she would find it quaint. Initially he had used it to tease, but in time it had become absorbed into their love-making. 'Tootsie,' he would sometimes murmur and kiss one breast. 'Wootsie' went with kissing the other. Ridiculous and sweet, the term and the accompanying actions were private to them. And 'toots' was the everyday version. But she did not want his sweet words, she did not want to remember how——

Hastily blocking the erotic thoughts, Keri made to march majestically out, but her exit lost its momentum when a sharp twinge struck at the base of her stomach. With a grimace, she halted mid-stride.

'Are you all right?' Shafe enquired, leaving his chair to come near.

'Never felt better,' she lied.

With a chin which grandly ignored his concern, Keri resumed her departure. Her insides might acknowledge the disastrous affect his words had had on her, but she would walk over hot coals rather than admit to any weakness.

'Honey, I realise life can seem like a bitch at times, but——'

She spun to him. 'Maybe newscasting is repetitive, yet plenty of people in television would kill for the chance you've been offered!'

'No kidding?'

'But then,' she continued scathingly, 'plenty of people would be content to lead regular lives with their families.'

Shafe's jaw hardened. 'Cheap shot.'

'You want me to apologise?' Keri demanded.

'I want you to get off my back.'

'Do you? Well, I want you to leap off the merry-go-round. Why you should regard newscasting as such an organic change, I've no idea. It's still television. It's still current events. It's still——'

Another twinge cut her short.

'Is anything wrong?' he appealed, placing his hand on her arm.

Keri shook herself free and straightened. Was anything wrong? What a dumb-fool question! Yes, something was wrong. Totally amiss. For example, him refusing to become orthodox. *And* them becoming embroiled in another stand-up row. *And* her stomach playing these painful games. But if Shafe couldn't work that out for himself, she was not about to tell him.

'Nothing's wrong,' she declared, swinging away.

When she disappeared into Emma's room, this time she took care to close the door quietly.

For two hours the 'nothing' in her stomach fretted and grumbled before finally subsiding and allowing her to sleep. When she awoke the next morning, Keri waited for a resurgence. It did not happen. Her head might be in turmoil—her immediate thoughts were of how infuriatingly uncooperative Shafe had shown himself to be—but her stomach remained calm. It was one thing to be grateful for amid what was fast becoming an avalanche of disasters.

Beside her Emma slept soundly, petal-soft cheeks flushed and rosy, so she devoted herself to some hard thinking. With unflinching honesty, Keri identified the minuses and pluses in her marriage. Minus number one, Shafe had been unwilling, or unable, to make love to her. Minus number two— since meeting her in Barbados he had not even *told* her he loved her. Neither had she said the words to him for that matter, but ... Lord, they really were strangers, weren't they? Minus number three—the crunch—he had thumbed his nose at newscasting. What *she* might desire did not count. He remained self-indulgently addicted to travelling the world.

With a dejected sigh, Keri moved on to the pluses. She cared about him, and cared deeply. Equally, signs existed which indicated that, strangers or not, lovers or not, he cared for her. But Shafe cared on the wrong level. His caring was loose, intermittent, of the 'now you see me, now you don't' variety. Her hackles rose. You could argue that an on-off husband and father was better than none, but—as Angela had asked on several occasions—was she prepared to settle for spasmodic visits from the man in her life, for the rest of her life? The answer was no! If she had had a tub handy, she would have thumped it. And not only did she refuse to lose out herself, but she demanded a better bargain for Emma. Her mother dying mere weeks after she had started school had taught Keri all she needed to know about the lack of a parent. It was a grievous gap in any child's life.

'Maamee?'

The sight of her baby smiling so happily, so innocently, so unaware, through the bars of the cot brought a lump to her throat and tears to her eyes. She lifted her out and sat her on her knee.

'Don't worry, my darling. I'll make everything perfect,' she whispered, resting a cheek against the fair, silken head.

Unreceptive to the moment of melancholy, Emma squirmed. A new day had dawned, and she needed to be off. She also needed to be changed, washed and dressed. With a sigh, Keri took her into the bathroom and set to work. As she had survived without her mother, so doubtless Emma would survive without Shafe's constant attendance, she thought as she dealt with the wriggling toddler— but why should she? Why should her daughter be expected to settle for second-best? Keri's jaw set rigid. It was clear that the time had come when she either shut up or spoke up. She intended to do the latter, forcibly. And if last night's argument appeared to have brought them to a dead end—well, Shafe would need to be persuaded into a U-turn.

This prospect proved so awesome that her stomach stopped behaving and gave one of its tender tweaks—something Keri was beginning to accept as a regular occurrence. Examined sober-mindedly, the likelihood of Shafe performing a U-turn seemed remote. He was very much his own man, a factor which, ironically, had contributed to her falling in love with him. His quiet independence had proved seductive.

Grimly she went through the motions of drying and powdering. If he had been debilitated the other night, serve him right! *If*? Keri hardened the word to 'when'. The reason he had failed to make love to her had to have been because he couldn't, not wouldn't. And the proof of that was, she argued, his vilifying her so-called crusade. What point would there have been in his objections if some other woman was lined up to bear the brunt of his truancy tricks? None. He would not have bothered—unless, feeling himself criticised, he had hit back simply for hitting back's sake? She buttoned Emma into a strawberry-printed dress and reached for the hairbrush. That was possible. And what about the other woman, was she a possibility, too? Up and down went her thoughts. In and out. Round and about.

Keri twisted a scarlet ribbon around the stalk of a tiny blonde topknot and tied it into a bow. This emotional schizophrenia was useless. It must be replaced by positive thinking. As Emma padded back into the bedroom in search of Baxter, she shrugged off her nightdress and stepped beneath the shower. She was *sure* Shafe had not cheated on her, and she was *certain* what had troubled him the other night had been no more or less than a physical malfunction. She reached for the soap. Doubtless, Shafe would have recognised his malfunction as temporary, but he would be desperate to know exactly how temporary. Afflictions which have a psychological root can often feed off themselves, and he might well be plagued with the fear of spending days, weeks or even months imprisoned in his own private hell. Keri raised her face to the water jet. She would rescue him, and when she did—her current determination refused to entertain doubts—wouldn't a combination of gratitude at having his confidence restored and the reminder of how pleasurable their lovemaking could be, propel him to alter his views on newscasting? As a resounding 'yes!' sounded in her head, Keri grinned. Her plans had not been wasted, they had simply been premature.

'Watch out, Shafe, I'm coming,' she murmured. 'And this time I shall swing things *my* way!'

Yet if she drowned him in her love and subsequently demanded the desired career change, wouldn't she be guilty of opportunism? Deep in thought, she rinsed herself off. Taking advantage of him in a weak moment would be unfair. The more honest approach would be to first root for her cause and then——

'Maamee!'

A shriek piercing the thrum of the water had her thrusting the shower curtain aside. Like all mothers, Keri could differentiate between a temper scream and one of distress, and she grabbed for a towel. Skidding wetly across the tiled floor, she dashed to investigate.

'Dadda!'

Shafe's appearance from the living-room had changed the cry.

'Never knew you were a mountaineer, ragtag,' he said.

Tears streaming down her face, Emma was straddling the cot headboard. Her chubby legs were stuck out rigidly on either side and two little hands were holding on for grim death. As he plucked the adventurer from her ledge, Keri came close, stroking and calming.

'She climbed up and was unable to climb down at my father's,' she told him, as the tears became snuffles and the snuffles dissolved into smiles. 'But because this cot is on a grander scale I presumed she'd think twice.'

'She will next time.' He removed a finger from an exploration of his ear and spoke sternly. 'You don't climb up there again. It's dangerous.' In reflex emphasis, Shafe tapped the toddler's leg. 'Understand?'

As taps go it was tiny, arguably a non-event, but Emma reacted as though he had wielded a cat-o-nine tails. Breaking into crimson-faced squeals, she writhed away.

'Maamee!'

'You stay with me and you calm down,' he said, restraining her. He glanced at Keri. 'Don't tell me you consider I'm the big, bad wolf, too?'

'No-o,' she faltered. Shafe had the right to a father's authority, and defining Emma's boundaries was no more than good sense, yet . . . She had been in sole charge for so long that now she needed to muffle the urge to clamp the child to her breast and order him to stop interfering. 'She isn't used to being scolded,' Keri said, in mitigation. 'Keeping the noise down was vital when my father was ill, so I tended to give Emma her own way. And afterwards——'

'Afterwards Angela wouldn't have been thrilled to have played hostess to a screaming brat?'

'No.'

Shafe stretched out his arms to suspend the toddler high above his head, an action which proved so surprising the squeals expired as swiftly as they had begun.

'You, ragtag, will not be allowed to develop into a young tyrant. Which means no more cot climbing and a little more give and take with poor Victor.' When he shook Emma, she gurgled with delight. 'You might laugh, but that ain't chopped liver, it's an order.' He brought the child down to his chest. 'I figure there'll be a few more reprimands before she gets the message, but when you consider her parentage, it's no wonder she's a bit——' he grinned at Keri '—on the wild side.'

'Speak for yourself,' she retorted. 'I'm not wild!'

'Unconventional, then.'

'I'm not unconventional!'

Amused grey eyes slid down. 'You reckon most mothers tend to their children when they're dripping wet and beautifully naked?'

'I'm not—oh!'

In all the fuss, the towel so hastily grabbed, secured and encouraged to stay in place by a star-fished hand, had drooped. Now, although Keri continued to fasten it to her front, it hung in a sodden vertical fall which neatly exposed a perfect round breast on either side.

'Mmm, like it,' Shafe murmured, smiling at a diamond of water which sparkled on one pink nipple. 'Does my lady wish me to dry her? I'm willing to perform the service with a towel, or with my tongue, or——' impudently he fingertipped the droplet away '—use any other method she chooses.'

The flurry with which she started back and covered herself made Emma giggle.

'Shafe, your daughter is watching wide-eyed and listening to every word,' Keri hissed.

Debilitated he might be, but he had lost none of the ease with which he could arouse *her*. Her

breasts, she knew, were burgeoning. And a treacherous ache throbbed between her thighs. But, as
before, the timing was maddeningly, frustratingly
wrong!

'Not in front of the children? Ah well, suppose
we drive into Bridgetown this morning? From what
I saw yesterday it looked well worth a visit.'

Keri took in a breath. 'Bridgetown sounds like a
good idea,' she agreed.

Lord Nelson's bronze statue stared down from its
plinth, sanguinely surveying the sunny hustle and
bustle. Picturesque with white villas, green sav-
annahs and a winding river, the island's capital was
the focus of activity. Everything of any importance
took place here, though in a happy-go-lucky, typi-
cally West Indian way. Seafaring interests were ca-
tered for at the Careenage, where schooners lay
awaiting repair, while further along the quay, near
the bridge in the centre of town, tourism held sway.
Here visitors lazed outside cafés, watching boats
moor or set sail as the morning drifted by. To sip
a fruit juice as they basked in the shade of a striped
umbrella was sufficient for some, but others were
already tucking into plates of cold cuts or patties
or pizzas. On the main street department store
windows held a fascinating display of goods, though
for those who preferred outdoors shopping there
were the nearby markets. At one stall pineapples
could be prodded, at another a plump red snapper
selected, at a third Rastafarian moccasins examined and tried on for size.

Keri took Emma from the moke, and waited as
Shafe fixed the buggy. Her outfit of sleeveless van-
illa-coloured shirt and slacks, with espadrilles of

the same shade, was casual and geared for the heat.
Likewise her hairstyle. Swept into a ponytail which
had been tied with a pale length of chiffon, her hair
swung free from her neck.

'Off we go,' she grinned, depositing the child in
her chariot.

A rough itinerary had been gleaned from a guide
book, and after inspecting the Trafalgar Square
fountain they headed for the House of Assembly.
The stained glass windows were a focal point, but
they had barely had time to admire them before a
group of housewives pounced. This disturbance
proved to be a foretaste of things to come. If you
pushed a flaxen-haired, blue-eyed baby, progress
around Bridgetown was slow—but pleasant. Bajan
friendliness was hard to resist.

'Rarity adds value,' Shafe proclaimed as, after
a third delay, they made their way towards the art
and crafts centre.

As she slid her dark glasses up her nose, it struck
Keri that now was as good a time as any to restate
her case. She had decided that tackling him ver-
bally must come prior to approaching him physically, so why wait? There was nothing to be gained.
On the contrary, the sooner she cleared the practicalities, the sooner Shafe would be holding her in
his arms. She needed him to hold her, needed it
desperately. The longer they remained sexually in-
communicado, the greater her desire to be loved
became.

'That's a great motto,' Keri said, then added per-
tinently, 'though it's not so much a motto for you
as an edict, isn't it?'

He surveyed her with sombre eyes.

'You're speaking in riddles. What's on your mind?'

'The future. Our future.' As if notified by radar of a fraught moment, her stomach clenched and unclenched. 'This isn't a question of who wears the trousers, Shafe. It's a question of me being fed up with being...docile.'

'Docile?' he laughed. 'Jeez, that's the last way I'd describe you.'

'Co-operative, then,' Keri adjusted. 'It suits you to spend a considerable amount of time away. However, I wish to put it on record that the arrangement does not suit me.'

'You want me on call, day in, day out?'

'Why not? Other husbands are.'

'Not all, by any means. The absent husband is one of the perils of modern existence. For example, what about the airline pilots, international businessmen, guys in the Armed Forces?'

Keri scowled. 'That's different.'

'How?'

'Well——' Behind her sunglasses, she scowled again. So engrossed had she been in *her* predicament, she had given not a single thought to others. 'Well——'

'If you required the model mate you'd have done better to have married a bank clerk. Or a features editor,' he added sourly. 'As I remember it, your good friend Larry Roach works to the kind of strict routine you can set your watch by,' he said, when she looked puzzled. 'In the office at eight-forty-five sharp, eat lunch in precisely fifty minutes, and clock off on the stroke of five-thirty. Catch train, which lands him back at his bachelor abode at six-fifteen on the dot. Right?'

'I suppose so,' she agreed, bewildered by Larry's sudden inclusion in their conversation.

'Keri, if you're figuring on getting around to that damned newscasting job, save your breath. As far as I'm concerned, the idea was unworkable nine months ago, and it always will be.'

'Always?' she said aghast.

'Yes!'

Before, she had listened to his denial of the job and reacted with horror, yet deep down she had not *believed*. Should she believe now?

'But——' Keri began stubbornly, then grimaced. 'Would you mind if we make for that bench over there?' For the past weeks the twinges in her abdomen had come and gone at random, but this morning the clenching and unclenching seemed horribly regular. The unrelenting rhythm was weakening her legs, making her light-headed. With a sickly smile of relief she sat down. 'I can't go on,' she declared, deciding to skip preliminaries and get down to the nitty-gritty. The fingers she raised to her brow met skin clammy with moisture. Despite the heat, she had broken out into a cold sweat. Keri shivered, feeling chilled yet feverish at the same time. 'I can't go on,' she repeated dizzily, and blinked.

Maybe her stomach's misbehaviour the previous evening should have warned that her physical state worked in sympathy with her emotions, but she had never imagined that when she next embarked on her 'crusade' she would be brought within shouting distance of collapse.

'Is something the matter?' Shafe asked, examining her pallor with worried eyes.

'Ha!' Intended to be heavy with derision, the laugh emerged squeaky and nonsensical. Keri pushed a hand against her side and did her best to concentrate. 'You're not claiming ignorance?'

'Honey,' he said tenderly, 'please would you tell me what's troubling you?'

In confusion, she gazed at him. She could not fathom out how or why, but they seemed to be talking about two different things. At cross purposes. At odds. Getting her message across was proving to be increasingly difficult, and now she wondered why she had begun such a conversation in a public place. Keri wiped a wet palm on her hip. If only she could think up an excuse for not continuing. But Shafe was sitting on the edge of the bench, scrutinising her as he waited for an answer.

'It's to do with you and me.' She noticed how Emma had twisted around in the buggy to look up at her. 'And our baby.'

'You mean you're pregnant?' he exclaimed.

Keri produced another nonsensical squeak. 'How could I get pregnant when you're never there?'

'It would be possible,' Shafe muttered. He brooded for a moment, then threw the thought away. 'Be fair. I'm not *never* there. Think back beyond these past four months and you'll recall——' He broke off to place his hand on her brow. 'Honey, you're burning up. You need a doctor. We passed a hospital on our way into town. I'll take you there. Will you be OK while I go back for the moke? I'll be as quick as I can.'

The dazed time during which he was gone stretched over a decade. The pain in her stomach was growing meaner by the minute. It had to be more than nerves—perhaps it was something she had eaten? Aware of a small dark woman in a maroon dress exclaiming over Emma, Keri found it impossible to reply. All she could do was hold an arm protectively across her stomach and hope the admirer mistook her grimace for a smile.

How grateful she was when Shafe returned.

'I feel rotten,' she wailed, reaching out for him. She needed to be comforted. She needed to cling. 'Nauseous and shaky, and——'

A jab had her doubling over, and then she was whisked up as he lifted her into the moke. The next thing she knew they were driving along, with a breeze blowing through her hair and red-hot pokers stabbing at her insides.

'The hospital,' Shafe said, when iron railings appeared on the left-hand side of the road, and if he sounded relieved Keri felt like weeping with thankfulness.

Behind the railings stood a white, three-storey building surrounded by cut lawns and flower beds. Pushing a 'stand clear' hand towards the guard who peered from a gatehouse, Shafe sped past and on, squealing to a halt beneath a portico.

'Stay where you are,' he instructed as he leapt out.

Keri gave a ghost of a smile; the last thing she could have done was go exploring.

A plaintive 'Maamee?' from behind reminded her Emma was in the moke, but she could not turn, could not reply. The pain eclipsed everything.

'I think it must be food poisoning,' Keri managed to say when Shafe appeared with a white-coated doctor by his side.

She was wrong. In less than two minutes, acute appendicitis had been diagnosed.

CHAPTER FIVE

WHEN Keri was lying down, she was fine. Likewise when she was standing up. The difficult bit was transferring from one state to the other; that demanded time, care, and an incredible amount of face-pulling.

'Straighter,' ordered Dr Baptiste, a slim, soignée negress who stood tall as a willow in her white coat. 'Shoulders back, now strut.'

'Strut!'

Chocolate-brown eyes gleamed. 'Dance the Funky Chicken if you'd rather.'

'Please don't make me laugh,' Keri begged.

'Spine erect. Pretend you're one of the guards at Buckingham Palace.'

She did her best, though as far as playing soldiers went she felt more like an ancient and invalided member of the Chelsea Pensioners than anything else. Demanding she rise from her bed the first morning after her operation might be normal procedure, but to Keri it seemed little short of barbaric. And she classed expecting her to *walk* as one hundred per cent sadism!

'Neat little scar you've got there,' the doctor continued, grinning mercilessly. 'Two inches or thereabouts and tucked below the bikini line.'

'Thanks,' she winced.

'My pleasure. You're bearing some exquisite embroidery, though I say it myself. Pity it'll be removed in ten days' time.'

'I'm to be discharged then?'

The young woman hooted with amusement. 'Lawdy, no! We kick you out in another four or five, then you return to the clinic for the stitches to be removed. Having an appendix detached is no great shakes these days.'

Keri grimaced. 'I'm glad you told me.'

'Let's stroll to the french windows and back again,' Dr Baptiste suggested, taking up the position of partner as her patient hobbled off.

The ward was wide and sunlit. Glimpses of the palms out of doors, allied with swags of exotic flowering creepers which peeped in at every window, imparted a pleasant 'tropical garden' feeling. Painted lemon and with ceiling fans which revolved slowly to stir the air, the room contained ten beds. Each came equipped with a yellow cover and a wooden locker which stood alongside. On the lockers vases of flowers and get-well cards were displayed. Despite her brief time in residence, even Keri had her share. Shafe, visiting the previous evening when she had still been dopey from the anaesthetic, had arrived with Emma tucked under one arm, a sheaf of red roses under the other.

'What's it like being married to a guy with a high PQ?' Dr Baptiste enquired, as they passed the refectory table where patients fit enough to be up and about had congregated.

'PQ?' she asked, returning the smiles.

'Personality quotient rating. According to an article I read in the States, your husband's in the throes of establishing himself as the kind of individual everyone would feel happy to have around. I received my training at medical school in California and, from time to time, return to visit friends,' her companion explained. 'I watch some television when I'm over there, so when I met your husband yesterday I thought his face seemed familiar. Later it clicked, and checking out the name clinched it.' She chuckled. 'I bet *your* eyes never glaze over with boredom?'

'They haven't done lately,' Keri agreed crisply, executing a cautious turn as she reached the glass doors which stood open at the end of the ward.

'I dare say he'll spend a fair amount of time in foreign pastures, but the periods when you have him home must more than compensate. Twelve days with a sparky guy is better value than twelve months with a dull one. I learned that from bitter experience.' Dr Baptiste groaned. 'I gave six of the best years of my life to a fella who regarded swapping baseball scores as the high point of any conversation. What a schmuck! He was always around, but ' her dark eyes rolled '—how often I wished he wasn't! There were times when I'd have sold my soul for a break.'

'But if he had been sparky, you'd have wanted him there all the time,' Keri attested.

'Live in each other's pockets?' The woman shook her head. 'There are couples who can function like they're Siamese twins and be deliriously happy, but most of us need some space. I know I do. I reckon there's a lot of truth in the saying that absence makes the heart grow fonder. A bit of separation does no marriage any harm. In fact, it can be as beneficial as a shot in the arm. You may take a rest now,' she said, as they arrived back at their starting point, 'but I'm leaving instructions with Sister that you're to exercise again later.'

Exhausted by her excursion, Keri perched on the side of the bed. Painstakingly she swivelled and, once aboard, eased herself back against the pillow, inch by geriatric inch. So Shafe was being lauded as the kind of guy everyone would feel happy to have around, was he? Oh boy, if only they knew how seldom he *was* around! If only they knew how one-directional he could be.

'I understand you've fallen ill on your holiday. That was bad luck,' a soft West Indian voice commiserated, and Keri turned to find the plump, grey-haired woman in the next bed smiling at her. 'How long have you been in Barbados?'

'This will be my fourth day.'

'So you'd barely had time to start enjoying yourself before you were rushed into hospital,' her neighbour murmured, tut-tutting in sympathy. 'I sure hope it won't be a case of boarding the plane for home the minute you're back on your feet?'

'No. I'm staying here for six weeks.'

The woman grinned. 'Then all is not lost. My name's Agatha, by the way.'

'And I'm Keri. Have you been in hospital long?'

'A fortnight and three days.'

If Baz Guiler had been a prolific raconteur, the minutes which rolled by indicated that in Agatha he had met his match. She talked about her operation to remove kidney stones, a subsequent ailment, her hoped-for recovery, and then—barely pausing for breath—moved on to tales of her family. Particular emphasis was given to her twelve grandchildren, the apples of her eye. The four girls and eight boys stretched from a twenty-year-old down to a babe-in-arms, and each one's life story was recounted in detail.

'I couldn't help noticing your little girl yesterday,' Agatha said, packing away a thick envelope of photographs, all of which had needed to be admired. 'She must be around the same age as my Wendell's Lorraine. Too tiny to understand what's happened to her mammy.'

'Er, yes,' Keri replied.

Emma—oh heavens! Her heart quaked. How it had happened she did not know, but in all the hours since waking—and it had been a dawn start—she had not given her daughter so much as a thought. How would Emma be faring without her? she wondered tardily, uneasily, worriedly. As far as last night's befuddled state allowed her to recall, at visiting time the toddler had been her usual merry self: wanting to get down, demanding to be lifted up, crawling over Shafe and never still for a minute. She had departed, flapping a vague but happy hand, and for Keri that had been that. It had never occurred to her to wonder about Emma's welfare, either physical or emotional or both. Instead there had been the unconscious assumption that any gap in the little girl's world would be filled by Shafe. That he would continue her routine. That his presence would keep her secure. But throughout their daughter's entire life he had disappeared for stretches long enough to classify him as a missing person!

Keri fussed with the lapel of her lavender silk robe. Agreed, since father and child had met at the airport a camaraderie had existed, yet what did that prove? Emma, pint-sized minx that she was, already exhibited a profound liking for men and possessed an astute eye for the more attractive of the species. Hadn't she set up a mutual admiration society with

Larry? Hadn't she flirted with him, grabbing at his spectacles and causing havoc with the neat knot in his tie? And, inconsistently, hadn't she turned the cold shoulder minutes later and demanded he release her to the comfort of her mother's arms?

Suppose the same thing had happened yesterday evening? Suppose, on their return to the bungalow, Emma had abruptly, heartbreakingly, realised she wasn't around? Bedtime, brimful of comforting ritual with the cuddles, the tucking in of the blankets, the final kiss on the nose, had to have been the testing time. Had she sobbed, had she screamed, had she refused to be placated? And if so, how had Shafe reacted? Keri's dismay billowed. While she did not doubt his affection, she could not help but doubt his competence. Used to a leisurely drink and a good book in the evening, how would he have coped with an intractable, hollering infant? He was a fair-weather father at best.

'I trust she isn't grieving for you,' Agatha murmured.

Hearing her fears voiced out loud, Keri shuddered. 'So do I.'

Visiting time took for ever to come, but the sight of Shafe walking along the ward, his hand held down to a staggery Emma, lifted Keri's spirits immediately. Far from being full of woe and fading away, her daughter looked joyous. And Shafe seemed encouragingly unruffled, too.

'Hi, honey,' he smiled, and raised the toddler to receive a kiss before he greeted her himself.

His kiss on the lips was friendly, but brief—too brief. It made no statement, and right now Keri was in dire need of one. Between exercising and resting there had been more than enough time to think, and fretting over Emma had been sandwiched with long periods when she had fretted about the future. Granted, her wayward appendix had ground her 'crusade' to a halt, but when she returned to it it would be with increased determination. There was no doubt, Keri had decided during the day's angst-ridden hours, but that she had been pressurised into an ultimatum. An ultimatum? She shrank away from the idea, but—like it or not—she must look him in the eye, and say loudly and clearly, enough is enough is enough.

However, she would play things differently next time around. Seduction must come *prior* to stating her terms, and to hell with charges of opportunism. All was fair in love and war, wasn't it? And the glaring truth was that Shafe, restored and relaxed, would be more receptive to her point of view. She had dallied with the idea before, then foolishly changed her mind. She would not change her mind again. Exactly when she would be fit enough to resume a love-life which, increasingly, seemed to have existed in the swirling mists of the past, was as yet unknown. However, Dr Baptiste had spoken of a tennis star who had leapt around the courts at Wimbledon two weeks after his appendectomy, so the date could not be too distant.

'Could I have another kiss?' Keri requested, determined that, hospitalised or not, in no way would she allow their relationship to dwindle further.

'Another?'

She smiled up. 'A better one.'

'Better?' Shafe repeated, as cautiously as if she was inviting him to commit a forbidden act.

'Here, I'll show you.'

Confident that the warmth of her embrace would work its own particular magic, she yanked on his arm and, as he bent, hooked an arm around his neck, drawing him down.

'Hey,' he protested when, despite Emma being between them and the flowers and packages he carried tumbling on to the bed, she pressed her mouth to his. Keri parted her lips, deepening the kiss. To the graze of his moustache against her skin was added the heady excitement of his tongue grazing hers. 'Hey,' he repeated, pulling away in a manner which left no doubt that if he had contributed, it had been only because he had been forced to. With a scowl, Shafe straightened, glancing hastily around. Several patients and their visitors had noticed the fervour of Keri's greeting and were smiling. He did not smile back. 'Maybe you don't mind providing the floorshow here,' he said in a steely undertone, 'but I do.'

She flushed scarlet. Never had she expected to be slapped down. Not for one moment had she imagined a mere *kiss* would be inadmissible.

'At—at the airport,' she stammered, 'you——'

'Entirely different,' Shafe denounced. 'Now you're lying in a hospital ward recovering from major surgery and surrounded by interested onlookers.' A curt gesture was made towards the gifts strewn over the bed. 'Suzette's sent home-made cookies. They come with her best wishes for a speedy return to perfect health.'

'Oh, thanks,' Keri said, and frowned. Maybe he had a point. Maybe in grabbing him so publicly into a clinch she could be accused of rash exhibitionism, but need he be so disapproving? 'How are you? How's Emma been?' she asked, struggling to ignore the numbing emptiness inside her. She gave her daughter a swift inspection. In blue and white striped dungarees and with her fair curls gleaming, the child showed every sign of being well looked after and content.

Shafe sat down beside the bed and pulled Emma on to his knee. 'She's fine, we're both fine, but it's you who's the invalid, remember? How are you feeling? I phoned in earlier and was assured you were making a good recovery.'

'I am, though I'm given no choice. They've had me walking up and down the ward enough times to qualify for entry in an Olympic marathon!'

He granted her a smile. 'Then you shouldn't be in here for long?'

'Not too long,' Keri said, and went on to relate Dr Baptiste's projected time-scale for her release. Talking—next she told him about the events of her day—acted as a balm and allowed everything to simmer down. 'It's a blow being in hospital instead of on the beach, but everyone's very friendly. The lady in the next bed, the one with the ranks of visitors, is called Agatha.' She broke off. A nurse had walked past, given a quizzical look, and was now marching towards the glassed-in office where she clearly intended to confer. 'Are you sure Emma's allowed to visit?' Keri queried.

'She has a special dispensation. Strictly speaking, kids under two are forbidden, but I explained to Sister yesterday that we were on holiday and how difficult it was to leave her with anyone.'

'You could have put her to bed early and asked Suzette to sit,' she pointed out.

Adopting a pained expression, he held Emma close. 'I prefer to have her with me. Besides, don't you want a visit from your baby girl?'

'Of course I do,' Keri declared, and gingerly leaned forward to receive a snuffly kiss from the special guest.

'According to the surgeon your appendix was in bad shape,' Shafe said, as his daughter slid from his knee and took a few tentative steps towards the end of the bed. 'He reckoned it must have been causing trouble for quite a while.'

Keri nodded agreement. 'I first noticed a pain in my side when I was looking after my father, but I put it down to stress—plus running up and down stairs so many times. After Dad died, I presumed everything would revert to normal and when it didn't——' her mouth made a downturn '—I attributed the blame to Angela.'

Aware of having handed Shafe a gift-wrapped opportunity to voice one of his anti-sister-in-law barbs, she waited—but she waited in vain.

'And when you arrived in Barbados and the pains continued, you attributed them to me,' he said, his voice as grave as his grey eyes. He tapped his knee. 'Come here, ragtag,' he instructed.

Emma, who had inched away until she had reached the aisle, was watching a pig-tailed girl of around six run and slide on the polished wooden floor. It looked a great game. One which two could play. At the sound of Shafe's voice she turned, plump lower lip thrust out. The pros and cons of rebellion were lengthily weighed before she tottered forward to lean against his leg.

'There you go,' he praised, bending to her.

'Dadda,' said Emma and clung tighter, though it was not so much cuddles she craved as something to hang on to and climb around.

'Who was it you interviewed in the Lebanon?' Keri enquired, using the diversion to change the subject.

Her stomach trouble and how she had related it to him needed to be discussed, but not now. Dive into such a topic and she would be up to the eyebrows in her ultimatum. No, thanks. Hadn't she decided she would demand the denouement of his travelling, a shift in his attitudes, only *after* their physical harmony had been restored? Keri threw him an uneasy glance. Earlier, restoration had seemed automatic; now his abhorrence of that one kiss set her wondering.

Shafe gave a grunt of surprise. 'A politician and a couple of religious leaders,' he replied, following on with their names and brief, potted biographies. 'As usual, all three held entirely opposing views on who's responsible for the situation over there. Why?'

'It's interesting. History at first hand. Had you met them on your previous visit?'

'Just the politician, though I shouldn't say *just*, because he was the guy who negotiated my——'

'Your what?' she enquired, when his voice tapered off.

'My release.'

'Release? Release from what?'

There was an awkward pause and then he flexed broad shoulders. 'The previous time I was in Beirut a group of Druze rebels got a hold of me.'

'Oh, my God!' Keri exclaimed, her eyes stretched wide with horror.

He had been captured? By rebels? Visions of Shafe gagged, in handcuffs, being knocked around, made her blood run cold. No wonder he had shown signs of disturbance when the Lebanon had been mentioned a day or two ago.

'There'd been a mix-up and I was mistaken for some other poor devil. The politician secured my freedom. It didn't take him long. In fact, my capture and release took place in less than an afternoon. I got lucky at just the right time.'

'But what—what did the rebels do to you?'

'Took me into a square and put a pistol to my head.'

Keri gulped. That did not sound like lucky to her. 'You thought you were going to——' she gulped again '—die? It must have been dreadful!'

'The air did seem a little thin for a while.' He raised a cryptic brow. 'I was grateful to be excused a repeat performance last weekend.'

'Shafe, when you came back from Lebanon the first time I *asked* what had happened, but you brushed me off! How could you do that?' Keri demanded. An enquiring glance from one of Agatha's visitors told her she had shrilled, and she lowered her voice. 'How could you keep quiet about something so serious?' she hissed.

'Do you know when it was you asked me? After I'd been home one whole week!'

She flinched at the hurt she saw in the tight line of his mouth.

'Was it?'

'Yes.' Shafe's tone was rough, as though it came from a sore part of his throat. 'I flew back to New York desperate to tell you, *needing* to work the experience through, but the first time I started to talk

Emma cried and you dashed off to deal with her.
When you returned you were full of some tale about
her having a cold and losing half a pound in weight.
Which she had regained, I hasten to add. It seemed
as if you didn't give a damn about what had been
happening to me and I thought, what the hell! On
the next occasion when I broached the Lebanon,
you gave a distant smile and went to feed her.
Whenever I tried, it was more of the same. The
baby. The baby. If you weren't attending to her,
you were talking about her, thinking about her. I
had to work so damned hard to gain your attention. Admittedly when I did manage it things
were fine, but the effort involved——'

'You never seemed particularly interested in
Emma, and I wanted to share what she'd done with
you, tell you what stage she was at,' Keri said, her
gaze on the bedcover. 'To me, each progression was
of the greatest importance.' Slowly her eyes met his.
'My priorities were wrong.'

'We were both at fault. You're right, I dis-
sociated myself from Emma when she was small. I
shouldn't have done. It was a big mistake.'

'But I made an even bigger one, didn't I?' she
said, after a moment of silence. 'Forgetting to take
my birth control pills nine months earlier.'

His brows came low. 'Keri, our honeymoon was
all heady excitement and no routine. We were so
head over heels in love neither of us thought
straight. Forgetting the pills was an accident, not
a mistake.'

'There's a school of thought which states no accident is accidental.'

'Hogwash! The decision we made to wait a couple
of years before starting a family had been mutual,'

Shafe said firmly. 'Becoming pregnant was the last thing on your mind.'

Sneaking a look around the nearby beds, Keri was relieved to see that no one was listening. A hospital ward was not the place for reviewing their private lives, yet they were deeper into a discussion than they had been for ages. And she did not want to stop talking.

'Things would have been different,' she suggested hesitantly, 'if—if I'd had an abortion.'

As though afraid the bogeyman might pounce, Shafe grabbed the child playing at his knee and lifted her on to his lap.

'What a dreadful idea!'

'Don't sound so indignant. Your initial reaction when we discovered I was pregnant was, well——' Keri frowned, remembering the conversation which had intermittently haunted for the past two years. 'You said there were ways round it.'

'Let's put that into context. You were complaining about being forced to give up your photography just at a time when you were making contacts and establishing yourself in New York,' Shafe said, showing by his total recall that the conversation had mattered to him, too. 'So yes, I said there were ways round it, meaning we could employ a nanny.'

'A nanny?' Perplexed, she looked at him. 'But I thought, I've always thought, you were suggesting I terminate the pregnancy.'

'Sure. I know.'

'Then why didn't you set me straight?' Keri demanded, thinking of how she had rounded on him that long-ago night. 'I accused you of wanting to kill your own child, and you never said a word. You never protested.'

'I kept quiet because, although becoming a father so soon was one hell of a shock, I wanted the baby. But——'

'But what?' she asked, when he faltered.

'But I doubted whether you did. Up to that point you'd been grousing like crazy and appeared——' Shafe tipped a hand to right and left '—uncertain about what you truly felt yourself. My remark concentrated your mind in one second flat. You came at me like a wild animal fighting for the survival of its young, and there was no more grousing after that. No indecision. Just full-scale commitment.'

'You genuinely wanted Emma?'

'Did I act as though I didn't?'

'No, you seemed thrilled,' she had to confess. 'But——'

He kissed the flaxen head of the child who had slumped against his chest, sucking her thumb.

'Keri, you were only twenty-four when she was conceived, but I was over thirty. Most of my contemporaries already had a child, if not two. I felt a sense both of time running out and me missing out.'

A minute or two passed as she pondered on this revelation. 'But if you were so eager for us to have Emma, how come you've never——' She stopped, unsure as to how to proceed with what could only be a condemnation. 'Why don't you——'

'Why have I just played at daddies ever since?' Shafe said, rescuing her from her dilemma.

'Yes.'

'Partly because trying to do my job the best I can and being Father of the Year all at the same time is not easy. Opportunities to get to grips are rare.' He paused, his face taking on a shuttered look. 'But also because——'

A bell rang.

'Two more minutes, visitors,' called the Ward Sister, her navy blue bosom quivering with importance.

'I'm getting to grips with Emma now,' Shafe declared, as a final rushed hubbub arose from the bedsides. 'These past twenty-four hours have been some eye-opener. I never knew looking after a kid was such a complicated business. Not only do you need to be on the alert every single minute, you have to be continually one step ahead.' He grinned down at his drowsy daughter. 'I'd also never realised that such a small child would be capable of learning things at such an amazing rate.'

'Like what?'

'One of the toys I bought is a jigsaw, the fitting wooden shapes into the correct place type. All it took was two demonstrations and Emma'd worked out what went where. And after doing it just once with Victor, she now knows how to play ring-o-roses.' He leaned back in his chair, pleased and proud. 'She went into the sea today without a hint of fear. There can't be many kids her age who——'

Keri laughed at his paean of praise. 'Stop it, you're beginning to sound like me.' Her amusement faded. 'How was she at bedtime? Did she cry?'

'Nope. Just settled down and went to sleep straight away.'

Keri knew she ought to be pleased that Emma had readily accepted Shafe as a replacement so rapidly, and she was—but it hurt not to be missed just one tiny bit.

'So I'm redundant,' she said, masking her regret with a smile.

'Let's just say you don't need to worry. Emma's being regularly fed and watered, and the two of us are getting along fine, aren't we, ragtag?'

As he was beaming at his daughter and she was beaming at him, a second bell rang.

'Visitors *out*!' ordered the Ward Sister.

In the midst of goodbyes Keri caught at his wrist, detaining him.

'Shafe, after such a bad experience in the Lebanon, why did you go again? Surely the network could have sent someone else?'

He sighed, positioning Emma more securely against his chest.

'I wanted to go. To be honest, I insisted. You see, I'd conceived some screwball idea about——' he searched for words '—facing up to the demons and exorcising them, I guess. I flew out of Kennedy bursting with bravado, but on the plane I began to wonder what in hell's name I was doing. Bad enough to dice with danger if I'd been a bachelor, but as a family man it seemed downright irresponsible.' His tongue sneaked out to moisten his lips. 'The gods wreaked their justice, because I ended up being terrified the whole of the time.'

'Out, *now*!' came the bellow.

'I'd better go before I'm terrified again,' he said, as the Sister marched up the ward. 'See you tomorrow evening. Same time, same place?'

'I'll be here,' Keri said wryly.

*　*　*

The next day her wound was less swollen, less tender, and walking up and down the ward came easy. The Funky Chicken might have been ambitious, but she could have handled a waltz. Indeed, Keri felt like dancing, and the reason was Shafe and Emma's growing affinity. Her disappointment at not being missed had rapidly been replaced with pleasure. How many times had she longed for him to forge a link? How often had she wished they were close? Now it was happening. And, as if this was not enough, in a moment of elation she had recognised a bonus!

Shafe's enchantment with a child who was accommodatingly, and with expert timing, showing herself to be alert, fearless and utterly congenial had added a vital dimension to Keri's 'crusade'. Previously the thrill of watching his daughter grow, of recording milestones in her development, might not have seemed special, but all of a sudden he *cared*. Now he took pleasure from simply being with Emma. Now he was involved. And, as a father smitten with his child, how would he be able to resist the logic that by becoming a newscaster he would be able to live with his wonder girl day-in, day-out? Keri smiled happily. The time when Emma's inclusion in her arguments had been little more than a moral, 'how can anyone allow their daughter to grow up without them' kind of appeal, was over. Now the plea carried an intoxicating weight of personal emotions. So much for her flailing around for ways in which to beach him; a baby blonde had hooked her sticky little fingers into his hair and was effectively dragging him ashore. Now her ultimatum could be reduced to the far more agreeable level of solid bargaining. Thank goodness!

To her surprise, when Shafe strode into the ward that evening he strode in alone.

'Emma fell asleep over dinner,' he said in answer to her query. 'Suzette's babysitting.' He bent to kiss her—on the lips and briefly, though this time she knew better than to ask for more—then took a small brown paper packet from among the miscellany of items he had placed on her locker. 'Shell earrings, from Captain Smiley. He noticed you weren't brightening up the beach and wanted to know why,' Shafe explained, as she unwrapped and admired the gift. 'That bikini of yours appears to have made quite an impact.'

'It won't be long before I'm wearing it again,' Keri told him, the gleam in her eyes betraying her glee. 'Guess what, Dr Baptiste was round an hour ago and she says so long as my wound remains clear I can leave tomorrow.'

'That's quick.'

'A result of the hospital being short of beds.'

'A result of you being young and healthy,' he substituted, dropping down on to the chair beside her.

'You make it sound as though you're ancient,' Keri rebuked.

'I feel it. I've got a four-aspirin headache, a damaged leg and my back's so bloody stiff I could play Quasimodo without trying!'

'What have you been doing?' she enquired, giving him a searching look. Often, on his return from long-haul trips, the stretch of skin across his cheek-bones and a faint mapwork of lines around his eyes, would give evidence of Shafe's weariness. She saw that weariness now.

'*I've* not been doing anything. It's your monster of a daughter who's responsible! Jeez, she's led me a dance.' He stared morosely down the length of his legs. 'Last night I said goodnight, downed half a tumbler of Scotch and fell into bed. I was dead beat, and I presumed Emma would be, too. She hadn't stopped moving the entire day and coming here to see you meant it was long past her bedtime. I was almost asleep when I heard a bloodcurdling yell. It sounded as though King Kong had broken into the bungalow and was all set to eat her alive. I leapt up, raced into her room, and what do I find?'

'Emma trying to climb out of the cot?'

Shafe growled in disgust. 'There she was, stuck on the headboard again.'

'You did say there'd be a few more reprimands before she got the message,' Keri reminded him.

'But what a damn fool thing to do in the dark!'

'She's only a baby.'

'I hurt my leg real bad,' he complained. 'You know the chest in her room, the one which has drawers with a yellow-metal corner trim?' She nodded. 'Well, one of the drawers had been left open and I charged straight into it. The trim was loose and it ripped my shin to pieces.'

His plaintive tone made it impossible not to smile.

'Sounds like the two of you are babies.'

'It wasn't funny,' Shafe rasped. 'And neither was the rest of the night.'

'Emma kept you awake?'

'She must have kept the entire western seaboard of Barbados awake! I'm surprised I wasn't deported this morning for harbouring an undesirable alien.'

Keri sobered. His outrage made it plain he regarded his daughter's behaviour as both inexcusable and a personal affront. Overnight the child who had enchanted had been revealed as a good-for-nothing, and a loudmouthed one at that. Fatherhood had ceased to be a joy. He was right, this was not funny, she thought in dismay. Not when it put her bargaining in jeopardy.

'You scolded her for climbing?' she enquired.

'I said she mustn't do it again, but I spoke pleasantly. I was also careful not to tap her leg. *And* I didn't swear, though with the blood trickling between my toes and my shin hurting like hell, God knows, I could have delivered a mouthful. Then the cries for "Maamee" started.' Shafe slung her a dark look. 'All of a sudden Emma had realised you weren't around. What's more, she'd decided the blame lay with *me*.'

'She wouldn't let you comfort her?'

'Are you joking? She glared at me through her tears and pushed me away, shrieking no, no, no. You said she could be hostile to strangers, but you'd have thought I was her worst enemy!'

'It would have been delayed reaction,' Keri soothed. 'OK, you're not a stranger now, but—but she doesn't really know you all that well, does she?'

'I'm her father!' Shafe protested.

'She must have worn herself out in time?'

'After what seemed like hours, she did agree to stop crying, but would she lie down in her cot?' He emitted a terse snort of a laugh. 'Fat chance! As fast as I tucked her in she scrambled up again.'

'Wouldn't you have done better to have simply left her to it?' Keri suggested.

'I couldn't. I might have rated lower than worm in her estimation, but she wasn't going to let me leave her. Not on your life! All it needed was me to so much as glance towards the door, and Emma held her breath and psyched herself up for another scream. I thought about her turning blue and going into a convulsion or a fit, or something. I agree she's never had one this far, but——' Shafe spread his hands. 'My leg was in a pretty sorry state, so I had no alternative than to take her around the house with me while I cleaned it up and found plasters. When we returned to the bedroom she created another scene. Even the damn cot had become a no-no now. I paced the floor with her for close on an hour trying to persuade her, but she refused to go back into it.'

Keri felt a lurch of compassion. 'What did you do?'

'What could I do, but take her into bed with me?'

'Did Emma go to sleep then?'

'Not until the early hours. She was lucky.' He tapped his chest. 'It was this jerk who lay awake!'

'You were too tense to settle?'

'No! I deliberately kept my eyes open because I was frightened that if I did go to sleep I might roll over and suffocate her, or fling out an arm and——' An elbow jolted, demonstrating the infliction of a black eye.

'But if Emma was out for the count, couldn't you have lifted her back into her cot? I've done that before, many times.'

'And risk waking her up?' he demanded, appalled. 'Keri, even moving seemed fraught with danger, so I lay there, stiff as a board and suffering all kinds of cramps.'

'Visitors out!'

The earlier bell had already rung and now the Ward Sister was on to her final call.

'How's Emma been today?'

'So hale and hearty you wouldn't believe!' Shafe said with a scowl. 'That I was Public Enemy Number One is now forgotten, so I've been pulled here, instructed to go there. I've done my best, but it was bloody hard work.' He rose to his feet. 'I'd better go.'

'I hope you have a peaceful night tonight,' Keri said, after hurried arrangements had been made for him to collect her the following day.

'Not as much as I do,' he muttered.

'Never mind,' she said, her smile a shade strained, 'if the worst comes to the worst, just remember you only need to last out until noon.'

Shafe glowered. 'I hope I make it. I don't think I can stand much more. I really don't.'

CHAPTER SIX

KERI'S homecoming was a hectic, noisy and, it had to be admitted, wearing occasion. Shafe had brought Emma with him to the hospital—after the stories of her pining, their reunion had proved surprisingly low-key—but a sizeable reception committee awaited back at the bungalow. There were Suzette and Victor, both decked out in their best clothes, together with two large, grinning ladies wearing ornate straw hats. Introduced as Suzette's mother and her Aunt Vi, they had been roped in to help with what was mysteriously referred to as the 'celebration lunch'. Captain Smiley was on hand with a mate, while Pot Boo and Sharkey completed the line-up. The local grapevine had been working well! Everyone was so pleased to welcome Keri back, acting as though she had been away for four weeks instead of a bare four days, that demands for her attention were multiple and conversation energetic.

When Suzette clapped her hands and announced that it was time to eat, it became apparent that impromptu parties were a way of life on Barbados. There were no false protests of 'I ought to be on my way'; instead everyone contentedly assumed the status of invited guest and lost no time in tucking into the 'celebration lunch' which had been revealed as a vast creole buffet set out on the patio. Bowls of Callalou soup were served first, then followed a fervent invitation for plates to be filled from the selection on the table. There were dishes of baked pork, fried fish, lobster, accompanied by crisp salads and all manner of exotic vegetables. Suzette's mother had prepared calypso chicken, while, not to be outdone, her aunt had produced her own speciality, pepperpot stew.

'If you're to regain your strength, you must eat,' Aunt Vi insisted, her frown suggesting Keri could be less than one meal away from starvation. She ladled out a hefty helping of savoury rice. 'Try this.'

Wary of gobbling down too much, yet not wishing to disappoint the ever-watchful cooks, Keri tasted mouthfuls here and mouthfuls there. A verdict was expected every time, and every time it was a sincere 'delicious'.

'Dessert now,' ordered Aunt Vi and Suzette's mother in unison, and indicated a choice of coconut cream pie or marble cake.

Smiling, she shook her head. 'I'd love to, but——'

The protests and persuasion which followed failed. Although the bulky ladies were able to consume slice after slice, Keri could not eat another bite. She had reached her limit. By the time coffee arrived so had a second limitation—no longer could she decently contribute to the general chit-chat. An unforeseen and sudden draining of energy had left her listless, reduced her conversation to murmurs accompanied by spray-on smiles. Much as Keri appreciated everyone's bonhomie, she longed for them to be gone. But cups were drained, refilled and drained again, and still the visitors lingered. It was well after three before they departed, and Suzette and her relations began clearing away the debris.

'Some dose of socialising,' Shafe remarked, as laughter and the clatter of crockery sounded from the kitchen. 'You must be exhausted.'

'I'll survive.' Keri placed her feet on the low stool he had provided and leaned back in her chair. 'You know, when I received the all-clear I assumed it'd be a case of straight away resuming normal service, but——' she gave a whimsical grin '—maybe I over-estimated.'

'I reckon you did,' he said easily. He looked across to where Emma had squatted. Round blue eyes solemn and rosebud mouth pursed, she was engrossed in capturing a feather with two fingers. 'Seems to be a tricky business,' he chuckled.

Keri smiled her agreement yet, contrarily, his current affability towards the toddler brought memories of yesterday's criticisms to mind. In the quiet which followed, she began to brood. Today Shafe had played the role of 'dearest daddy' to the hilt. He had taken Emma around, kept watch, patiently fed her her lunch. And the child had been good-natured throughout. But how long would his play-acting last—she was convinced he must be acting—merely until another lapse? Would a tearful rejection, a stubborn refusal, another screaming match have him demanding to be released from his contract?

'I presume Emma slept last night?' she enquired.

'Twelve solid hours. Wonderful!'

'So now your daughter's back in your good books?' she said archly.

'She was never out of them.'

Keri did not believe him, just as she did not believe in the 'Emma' dimension any more. After his ranting and raving, the idea of using it to give added thrust to her bargaining had been scrapped. As the idea of bargaining *at all* had needed to be scrapped. She had been forced into a stance where, once again, the only course of action left open to her was an ultimatum. Her mouth went dry. If back-flips would have secured an alternative option, Keri would have willingly leapt backwards for mile after mile after mile. But there were no other options. An ultimatum it would need to be.

'Could you give me that in writing?' she gibed.

'But it's true,' he protested. 'A couple of nights ago was the first time I'd ever come up against——'

'For someone rejoicing in their offspring, you did a good imitation of being disillusioned,' she remarked drily.

Shafe jammed his lips together. 'I'd had a rough night. A fraught night. When I came to see you in hospital I was hung over, and so I guess I...mainlined on complaints. Now I've come to terms.'

Keri fingered an ear-ring. 'How's the injured leg?' she asked.

'Better. Look, in dealing with Emma you've had your moments of feeling boxed in, too. You've wanted to headbang and crawl up the walls. As I'm new to the game surely I'm allowed——' He broke off when she yawned. 'You need some sleep.'

She shook her head. 'Half an hour of peace'll see me recovered.'

'A nap,' he decreed.

'No, thanks.'

'Be sensible,' he coaxed.

'I am,' Keri retorted, bristling.

Not satisfied with insisting that his displeasure in their daughter had been insignificantly transitory—and that in being displeased he had been copying *her*!—Shafe was now insisting in other directions, too. Keri glowered. He could go and take a running jump!

'Not sensible enough.' A silencing hand was raised. 'I ought to explain that while you were getting changed this morning, Sister called me into her office. She felt it was important I know that, in her opinion, you've been discharged prematurely. Apparently she'd argued with Dr Baptiste, but was overruled.'

'My scar's almost healed,' Keri protested.

'Maybe, and maybe the Sister's views belong to the old school, but there's more to your state of health than a wound. Surgery is a shock to the system. It takes time to recover from a shock, and a good dose of restful serenity.'

'You gleaned that information from a tablet of stone, oh, great wise one?'

Shafe ignored her. 'Sister said for you to cut out non-essential activities, like lifting Emma. I'll organise a programme of excursions which'll take her off your hands for a while.'

Keri stared at him. 'You mean I'm to be left high and dry?'

'You'll get better quicker if there isn't a small child hanging around, continually making demands.'

'And I thought you couldn't wait to pass her back!' she retorted, and was once again ignored.

'Sister recommended eight solid hours of rest each night. I'll sleep in Emma's room. That way, you won't be disturbed.'

Throughout the conversation there had been tremors of disquiet, but now Keri felt as if she had been hit by a small, localised yet devastating earthquake. They were to inhabit separate beds *again*? But why? Why this determination to keep her at arm's length? Her heart pounded as, all of a sudden, the 'other woman' zoomed from being a faint possibility to a clear-cut probability.

'You won't disturb me,' she rushed to assure him.

'I might.'

'How? Unlike Emma, I'm a big girl, so if you fling out an arm, which you've never done in the past, it won't be fatal. And you're hardly likely to roll over and suffocate me,' she added, heartily wishing he would.

Whether or not being abolished from his bed was responsible, Keri did not know, but right now Shafe looked so desirable her palms itched. Days beneath the Caribbean sun had deepened his tan and, in contrast, his teeth were a dazzling white and his pale grey eyes shone with a magnetic brilliance. But if his looks made her gooey, his body held the power to drive her insane. While she was relatively formal in a *café au lait* shantung shift, his shirt and shorts were casual—and seemingly designed to remind her, as if there could be any doubt, that he was male, male, male. Her gaze slid from the open collar where golden hairs glinted, across the muscular contours of his chest, down to the firm, brown thighs revealed by his hip-hugging khaki shorts. Keri moved restlessly. Maybe it was inappropriate for her, a convalescent, to feel this way, but she wanted to touch his thigh. She wanted to smooth her hand slowly down his leg to his bare ankles, and up again.

'If Emma wakes in the night I shall attend to her,' Shafe said, using the voice of officialdom. 'And if we were in the same room, me switching on the light, getting in and out of bed, moving around, would be bound to disrupt your sleep.'

'I don't mind.'

'But I do,' he retorted. 'Barbados is a wonderful place for a vacation, and the sooner you're fit and well and fully able to enjoy, the better. You gain, everyone gains.' He threw her a glance. 'All I'm interested in is your speedy recovery, can't you see that?'

Keri gave a weak smile, and said nothing. As far as she could see, all he was interested in was handing her a leper's bell.

A routine was quickly set. Around nine they breakfasted, and after subsequently waving Shafe and Emma off—sometimes they went on the beach, other mornings they sped away in the moke—Keri would write postcards, read, or chat with Suzette. At one o'clock the wanderers returned for lunch. Over the meal their earlier activities were discussed, and then Shafe would shuffle the female members of his family off to their respective bedrooms. Invariably Keri slept the longest, sometimes for an hour or two, and when she awoke it was to an empty house. Late afternoon Shafe and his charge reappeared, and they shared what, for Keri, was the best part of the day. As streaks of gold, orange and pink filled the sky and gilded the smooth surface of the sea, they would stroll along the beach. Always there were diversions: a shell to be collected, a water-skier to be watched, the exercising beach boys to be marvelled at. Later, they returned to the patio to sip a glass of wine. Dinner followed, and when Emma had gone to bed they would play cards, or watch television, or bring out the Trivial Pursuit.

Though Keri was loath to appear too much the devotee, this regime suited her. Considering how uneventful the days were, it was astonishing how quickly they passed. Maybe she *had* left hospital too early for, no matter how bright-eyed and bushy-tailed she felt on waking, sooner or later she did feel tired. She did droop. The periods of tranquillity, initially regarded as equivalent to a prison sentence, were something to be thankful for.

She also gave thanks for the ease with which, despite their unresolved problems, she, Shafe and Emma melded into a family. The father who, not so long ago, had been a novelty was fast becoming an integral inhabitant of the little girl's world. With uncritical nonchalance, she allowed him to bath her, feed her, amuse her. Keri was grateful Shafe undertook these tasks, yet because she knew he did them for just one reason—to hasten her recovery—that gratitude could not help but be tainted. She found herself wondering if he might secretly be counting the days, the hours, the minutes, until he could hand over the reins. He seemed content, but how much of this contentment was counterfeit? Looking after a child had to be commonplace compared with reporting international events. The occasions when Emma kicked up and Shafe stayed cool made her suspicious, too. Like his contentment, the coolness appeared genuine, but knowing she expected him to complain, then he damn well wouldn't—would he?

By the end of the week the twitch in her side when she bent or swivelled had disappeared. Keri's afternoon sleeps grew shorter, short, tapered off altogether and time began to drag.

'I feel great. Fully healed and ready to take up where I left off,' she jauntily advised Shafe at breakfast one morning. 'So whatever you're doing today, count me in.'

He gave a stern shake of his head. 'We'll wait until you've had your stitches out, then we'll see about things.'

'Oh, will we?' she challenged.

'Yes!'

Keri made a grab for the percolator. She did not appreciate his stick-in-the-mud caution. Nor did she appreciate, 'We'll see about things'. Shafe made it sound as though he was content with the status quo and wary about—— She frowned, wondering exactly what 'things' referred to. Did he mean her sunbathing on the sand, or going around and about in the moke, or... them sleeping in the same bed? Cold fingers curled around her spine as the 'other woman' theory, which went up and down in her mind like a barometer, gathered a few points.

Charily she eyed him over her coffee-cup. He did not act like someone agonising over a clandestine affair—the gathered points fell—so if his attention was for her to continue spending the nights alone it could only be because he doubted his ability if they combined. Yet surely Shafe must realise that the sum total of what he would achieve by avoiding her was elongated anguish? And he *was* avoiding her. He might be friendly, supportive, a good companion, yet so far as any gesture which was remotely sexual went—forget it. Once, there had been

a time when he had been unable to move near
without a kiss or a caress, but now, apart from a
dutiful goodnight dab on the cheek, he never
touched her. It was as if he dared not lay a finger
on her flesh lest it burned him.

A couple of days later her stitches were removed
and Keri was pronounced fit.

'It's all systems go?' Shafe grinned, when she re-
joined him in the clinic's crowded lobby. Although
the wait had been less than fifteen minutes Emma
had fallen asleep and, as the child awakened, he
hoisted her against his shoulder. 'Great news!'

His pleasure sounded sincere, but Keri was dubious. Despite the smile, could he now be engaged in
concocting excuses for an on-going separation? As
they went out to the moke, she reached a decision.
Whatever his reasons, she would not stand for being
outlawed any longer. She *could* not stand for it.
She had never regarded herself as threaded through
with nymphomaniac tendencies, but that rest-
lessness whenever she looked at Shafe was becoming an urge increasingly difficult to control. All
it needed was for something to snap, and she would
be flinging herself on top of him and tearing off
his trousers! Tonight, the moment Emma was in
bed, there must be a showdown. She would demand
to be told her rating on his chart of women with
sex appeal. If she occupied first place, then golden
trumpets would fanfare and choirs would sing and
doves would soar in the air. If not—Keri refused
to think about that.

Nerves stretched to dental floss, she awaited
seven-thirty. *The moment Emma was in bed* arrived—but alas, Emma did not want to stay in bed.

For some upside-down reason, the shorter than usual nap on her father's knee had fouled up her sleep requirements and, instead of being tucked in as snug as the proverbial bug, she wanted to play. As she had done a couple of weeks earlier, Keri held her, cuddled her, gave her a drink, but as fast as she laid her down, Emma clambered up to grab hold of the cot rail and bounce. Her little face wreathed in smiles, she bounced up and down endlessly. A battle of wills developed, jovial on one side, frenetic on the other. Had her daughter been older, Keri would have resorted to blackmail and bribery—a chocolate bar if she would go to sleep, the promise of a trip to the zoo, maybe even a new bicycle? And if that had not worked, she would have been tempted to bind her hands and feet and apply a gag! As it was, all she could do was offer up fierce and silent prayers for Emma to co-operate *quickly*.

'You don't seem to be making much headway, so why not give her a free run for a while?' Shafe suggested, looking in. 'It could tire her out.'

'She ought to be tired out now!' Keri protested.

'Maybe, but her staying awake can hardly be classed as a disaster.'

'You're right. It isn't a disaster, it's a calamity! The time she refused to settle for you, you foamed at the mouth,' she reminded him tartly, when he looked amused.

'I trust you're not going to hold that against me for ever?' he said, and reached into the cot. 'This won't become a habit, ragtag, but now's your chance to grab yourself some exercise.'

Out on the patio the toddler pranced around in her peony-pink nightgown, while Keri kept a keen watch. At the first suck of her thumb, a rub of the eyes, she would pounce and whisk her back to bed. Yet although time passed, Emma resolutely showed no sign of flagging. Instead, she peered into plant pots, inspected the books on the table, and played princess, all the while towing around her fur seal which did duty as kneeler and height booster.

'I saw these in the local shop,' Shafe explained, returning with a packet of balloons. He selected a yellow snake and stretched it a few times. 'Maybe batting one around'll use up her surplus energy.'

'Or maybe not,' Keri muttered ominously. 'You never went wild, lavishing things on her before,' she commented, as he started to puff and the would-be recipient doddered over to watch, 'but now Emma must think every day comes complete with a gift.'

He gulped in air. 'I bought Baxter.'

'Not much else,' she said, grinning when, despite Shafe's frantic efforts, the balloon remained flat as a pancake. 'I realise go-go travel inhibits window shopping, yet——'

'My travelling was immaterial,' he panted. 'It was you who inhibited me.'

'Why me?' Keri queried.

'Because——' He paused for breath. 'Remember the wooden doll I brought back, the painted wooden doll?'

'The one I said I'd prefer Emma not to have because there was no way of knowing whether the paint contained lead?'

'Correct, except now you sound reasonable whereas then you——' Shafe refilled his lungs and blew again. Again nothing happened. 'I'm getting too old for this,' he declared, sagging. 'Then you were so bloody anti you made me feel like I'd deliberately set out to poison her!'

'But the doll could have been dangerous. It came from a Third World country, where rules relating to paint toxicity probably didn't exist. All I wanted to do was safeguard Emma.'

'Fine. And I should have known better, as I agreed at the time. Yet would you leave the subject alone? Would you hell! You were like a trading standards officer whose needle had stuck.' He raised the limp snake to his lips and blew for all he was worth. Suddenly it inflated into a yellow oval. A few more puffs, and the balloon was robust. Emma jumped up and down with glee. 'For days I was bombarded with tales of spikes discovered inside Jack-in-the-Boxes, glass eyes which had been swallowed, fluff which had lodged in some poor child's throat,' he chanted, tying a knot. 'After that, whenever the opportunity to buy something arose I thought once, twice, three times, and in the end decided to leave such matters alone. Here you go, ragtag,' he said, and flipped the balloon high in the air.

Open-mouthed, Emma watched, but keeping track demanded so much tilting and twisting that she went down on her bottom with a thump. Up she scrambled, eager to grab the prize the instant it floated down to earth. But the balloon had suspended itself on a thermal on the patio roof.

'I apologise for being so heavy-handed,' Keri said, and sighed. At the time, the determination to ensure her child's safety and welfare had dominated everything, yet now it seemed less paramount than paranoid. Though, she thought with a spark of recognition, in the paranoid department she had company. 'But being over-protective is an easy trap to fall into when you're a first-time mother, responsible for a tiny baby and——' she thrust in '—left on your own so much.'

Tardily the balloon had decided to descend, but Emma had misjudged her position. Arms wide, she was jiggling up and down in the centre of the patio, while an air current had drifted the balloon to one side. There was a pout, a squeak of dismay, then down on all fours she went, scuttling in pursuit with knees moving like pistons.

After enjoying the turmoil, Shafe grew serious. 'The first-time mother can also be snared by over-possessiveness,' he said, turning a deaf ear to the reference to *his* obsession: travelling. 'Something a first-time father finds hard to handle.'

'Does he?'

'Jeez, I've been bright green.'

Keri frowned at him, surprised. 'You were jealous?'

'Twice over. As if being jealous of the attention you gave to Emma wasn't enough, I was also jealous of the attention she gave to you. A love affair seemed to be taking place, one which left me playing gooseberry.'

'It was my fault. I was much too clingy. I've known that for a long time.'

Shafe's grey eyes probed. 'You have?' he asked, as though he did not quite believe her.

She nodded. 'When Emma was born, instead of keeping in touch with things which had previously interested me—my photography, your experiences, what was happening in the outside world—I settled for being a mother. Period. As you said, Emma was all I could see, all I wanted to talk about.' She pulled a face. 'How dull I must have been, yattering on and on about formulas and such!'

'Not dull,' he grinned. 'More like fanatical.'

'I never meant to exclude you, it just... happened.' Keri cast him a glance. 'But perhaps it wouldn't have done, if you'd shown more desire to become involved.'

'I know, I know,' he said, abruptly impatient. 'If I'd worked at it, Emma would have accepted me. Instead, when I didn't receive on-tap recognition, I took the huff and opted out. It was a juvenile reaction.' Shafe brushed a strand of hair from his brow. 'When we were talking about this before, I said there were two reasons why I only played at daddies. The first was shortage of time, but I ducked when it came to telling you the second one.' He paused. 'It's not easy to admit this, it sounds so...petty, but the main reason I chose not to make much of an effort was my resentment, my jealousy of the closeness the two of you shared. It underscored everything.'

Keri considered the revelation. That she had failed to understand how he had felt showed how dismally out of touch they had been. Aware of the past tense, she sat up straighter. *Had* failed. *Had* felt. *Had* been. Their discord must remain in the past. And she must clarify the present.

'You can forget about being jealous now,' she assured him earnestly. 'Emma's clearly stuck on you and, as for me—well, I think you're nothing less than edible. That being so, I was wondering if you——' She began to stumble. 'Keeping away from me when I was convalescing is one thing,

but ... well, do you want ... don't you? ... you do
still ... I mean——'

Her voice petered out. Shafe was not listening.
His attention had strayed to a corner of the patio
where Emma, having corralled her prey, was lying
beside it. With thumb in mouth and eyelids closing,
the picture she presented was of one sleepy little
girl.

'Phew!' he exclaimed, flicking invisible perspir-
ation from his brow. 'The impossible appears to
have happened.'

Keri grinned. After spending the evening on
tenterhooks, she had arrived at her *raison d'être*
and promptly been forestalled. It did not matter.
Not when she knew that any delay in confronting
Shafe must now be brief. Though maybe 'con-
front' was the wrong word? The way they had
talked over the past half-hour was significant.
Faults had been acknowledged on both sides, yet
instead of spitting at each other they continued to
communicate. It augured well.

When Shafe lifted the toddler a small hand
fumbled for the balloon, and it was being hugged
to Emma's chest as he laid her down in the cot.

'Goodbye, macho image,' he joked, kissing
goodnight to his daughter, Baxter, two teddies and
a lamb with one ear. He stood back. 'Your turn.'

Keri cheerfully obliged. They had retreated and
were almost at the door when Emma flung the fur
seal, trapped the balloon against the side of the cot,
and—bang! A split-second of stunned silence was
followed by the child's frantic shrieks and Keri's
heart plummeting. So much for a brief delay! So

much for an imminent confrontation! Ten minutes passed before peace was restored.

'Back to square one,' Shafe announced, as a wide-awake Emma once more bounced up and down.

Remembering his comment about headbanging and crawling up walls, Keri groaned. It demanded every ounce of her will-power not to succumb to both, now.

'Don't you dare suggest another balloon!'

'Wasn't such a bright idea, was it?' he admitted, shrugging philosophically.

'Not as it turned out. And if we attempt to leave her alone now, she'll scream the place down.'

Shafe rubbed at his jaw, thinking. 'We could give low cunning a shot.'

'How do we do that?'

'Stay put, but become tedious zombies. The idea being that when Emma realises there's no profit to be gained from staying awake, she'll zonk out.'

'And how do we become tedious?'

'You stretch out on the bed while I switch off the light,' he instructed. 'Emma, Mummy and Daddy are going to sleep and it's time for you to go to sleep, too.' He patted away an ostentatious yawn. 'Goodnight.'

Keri felt the mattress dip as he sat down, then he placed his arm around her shoulders and lay down, pulling her close. Her heart thumped so hard she was certain he must hear it, feel it. If Shafe had lain beside her in a suit of armour there would have been excitement enough, but all he wore was a short-sleeved shirt and his khaki shorts. The body parallel to hers was lean and strong and masculine. Her dress, a skimming chemise of pale aqua, had become as fine as gossamer. It offered no protection from the vibrancy of his flesh. His closeness intoxicated her senses, made her head spin, sensitised with all the potency of an electric current.

The touch of his hand on her knee, his fingers stroking the soft, tender curve behind it, held Keri rigid. Was this a knowing caress or some kind of reflex action? Bemused, she gazed at him. His head was only inches away on the pillow, yet with no light but the moonlight it was impossible to read the expression in the depths of his eyes. But she had to know. It was *vital*.

His hand, slightly rough and making her skin quiver deliciously as it journeyed beneath her skirt to caress her thigh, provided the answer. His kiss confirmed it. His lips touched hers, fleetingly for a moment, as though Shafe could have been seized by a sudden doubt, then he muttered something which was half a sigh, half a declaration of desire, and his tongue entered her mouth.

Keri revelled in his opulent exploration, in his fever, in his undeniable need. He tasted of nectar. And when eventually Shafe drew back to tantalise her lips, outlining them with the tip of his tongue, she felt as if she was spinning.

'You picked the right strategy,' she whispered, with a shaky quiver of a laugh. She looked beyond his shoulder to the cot where their daughter was slouched, sucking her thumb again and pummelling Baxter in a desultory manner. 'Emma thinks all this is extremely tedious.'

He locked her more tightly to him and the large hand on her thigh moved further, his fingertips pushing beneath the edge of her white lace panties.

'And what do you think?' Shafe murmured.

His hand had reached the curve of her buttock, where he was kneading and gently fondling, setting her afire.

'Why, I agree with Emma.'

'Toots, you're an atrocious liar. But you're also so bloody desirable I'm going mad wanting to feel your naked breasts, wanting to kiss the bush of curls between your thighs, wanting to burst into you. And if there's any doubt about that, give me your hand.' Shafe smiled through the darkness. 'I wouldn't want to be thought an atrocious liar, too.'

The proud maleness of him beneath her fingers sent a thrill piercing through her.

'You're telling the truth,' Keri managed to say.

'I want us to be naked. Soon. Soon. Soon.' Each time he whispered the word it gathered urgency. He flung back an exasperated glance. 'When is that kid going to go to sleep?'

'Soon, soon, soon,' she replied, dizzy with pleasure and able to tease. She placed a finger across his lips. 'Now be quiet and be still.'

'God, this is torture,' Shafe groaned. 'Keri, I want you so much I——'

'Shh.'

After that he was quiet and he was still, apart from his hand which was addicted to making seductive forays. Minutes later the thwacking of Baxter ceased and Emma settled on to her tummy. Hardly daring to breathe, they waited a second, an hour, a year, until her eyelids lowered and her lashes spread on her cheeks. As her thumb fell from her mouth, they rose and crept out. Kissing feverishly, they went to the other bedroom.

'Let me look at you,' Shafe begged, when they were both naked. His grey eyes travelled adoringly up and down. 'You're even more beautiful than I remember,' he sighed, cradling her head between his hands and covering her mouth with his mouth. 'Keri, I love you.'

'And I love you.'

There were more kisses. Open-mouthed kisses. Lips-sticking-to-lips kisses. Desperate kisses.

'You have no idea how often you've almost had the clothes ripped off you. And I've lost count of the number of times I've undressed you in my mind.' He drew his hands down the silky curve of her back, drawing her into him. 'Keeping my distance since you came out of hospital has been hell.'

Keri pulled back. 'You didn't act as though you were—as though you wanted me,' she protested. 'You acted like a brother!'

'So I'm in line for an Oscar.'

'There was no need to treat me like——' her rebuke contained a hint of a sob '—a leper. Even though it was too soon to make love, we could have shared the same bed.'

'No. No way,' Shafe objected. 'Honey, I couldn't trust myself. I was so ravenous for you it would have been impossible to lie beside you without *taking* you. You remember when I visited the hospital and you kissed me?'

'And you jerked back like you'd come into contact with a vampire?' Keri responded pertly. 'Yes, I do!'

'You know why I jerked back? Because the moment your mouth touched mine, it was instant and overwhelming arousal.' He made a fist. 'Kerpow! I wanted you more than I'd ever wanted you before, and I wanted you *then*. I was sure everyone around us must have known what was happening.' He shook his head in confusion. 'Toots, I went hot and cold.'

'Alert hormones are healthy hormones,' she recited, grinning.

'Healthy! They damn near had me walking out of the ward on my knees.'

Keri laughed, then became serious. 'Bed apart, you needn't have spent this last week being so everlastingly platonic. The odd kiss wouldn't have——'

'The odd kiss would have started something I would have been incapable of stopping,' Shafe insisted. 'I was so damned horny it had to be all or nothing.' He bent to nibble at her shoulder. 'I used to take making love in my stride, but lately I've been charging around like a bull on heat!'

'Moo.'

He chuckled and wound his arms around her. For a while they stood there, kissing with parted lips, running their hands over the other, learning each other's bodies again, until the need for greater intimacy carried them to the bed.

'A long time ago, in what seems like another lifetime, I told you I wanted to lick every inch of you,' he murmured, leaning over her. 'Now it's going to happen.'

Shafe took hold of her wrists and, stretching out her arms, gently pinioned her to the bed. Then his head came down and in soft sucks, tender bites, moist kisses, he began working his way down her body. Her throat and shoulders thrummed with his blissful caress and slowly, slowly his mouth reached her breasts. Keri strained to meet it. His tongue was flickering over her nipples again and again, bringing them to such exquisite tightness that she broke free of his hold in order to grasp her breasts in her hands and offer them up to him. His mouth covered the rose-red tips, creating a turbulence which washed down to her thighs like a hot, impetuous flood.

'Shafe,' she moaned.

He moved lower, until she murmured his name again and clung, her fingers tightly gripped on his shoulders, the nails biting in. His sensuous pilgrimage continued, down her thighs, to that vulnerable spot at the back of her knees, to her ankles and her toes.

'Time for the return journey.' He raised his head and grinned. 'Think you can stand it?'

'No.'

But she did—just. As his lips reached hers, Keri writhed against him. She had never felt so hot. She had never felt so moist. She had never felt so open. When he spread his hands at her waist and steered her over until she was looking down at him, for a moment she was startled.

'I do like a woman who's on top of things,' Shafe murmured, but as he parted her thighs his playfulness became grave pleasure. 'God, that feels so good.'

'Wonderful,' she agreed, her hips moving in the song of love.

'Slower, Keri. Slower,' he begged.

It was too late. He was caught in her rhythm. Inexorably it increased, until their harmony was one and they were gripping, clutching, their breath coming shallow and fast until, in one ecstatic, exploding moment, they cried out together.

CHAPTER SEVEN

'THERE was a time,' Shafe began stiltedly, 'when I very much doubted whether we'd ever make love again.'

After dozing, they had showered together and, an hour later, were back in bed.

'I know, and I'm sorry.' Keri smoothed her fingertips down his cheek in an attempt to eradicate the tension she had detected. That he should continue to fret *now*, after such bliss, was touching. 'Don't worry, darling, it won't happen again. I won't let it,' she murmured.

He pulled back to give her a look which managed to combine fury and incredulity in equal proportions. 'You're not—not saying I was right, after all?' he demanded.

'Right about what?' Keri asked, bewildered by this sudden blitz.

'You and Larry Roach.'

'Me and Larry?' she repeated dumbly.

'You had a goddamn affair, didn't you?' he slammed. 'Isn't that what you mean?'

'No!'

'Oh.'

'Wherever did you get such a ridiculous idea?' she enquired, as Shafe sagged back against the pillow, his anger defused as rapidly as it had exploded.

'It isn't ridiculous.'

'It is. Larry and I may be friends, but so far as anything more goes, forget it. He isn't remotely my type. It's tall, sexy Americans who turn me on,' she said, teasing the hairs on his chest. 'Or to be more precise, tall, sexy Americans called Shafe Rokeby.'

He caught hold of her hand. 'Keri, you went to Warwickshire with the guy.'

'Yes, but——' She broke off. 'How did you know about that?'

A pillow was thumped, and once he had settled himself against it, he began to speak. 'When I stopped off in London and heard you'd gone to the country, I decided to motor up and join you for a night. It was to be the——' Shafe made quotation marks '—big surprise. The neighbour didn't know your exact location, so I went round to see a couple of your girlfriends thinking they might be able to help. I called on Cathy and Tina, but both of them were out. Then I remembered Larry. You'd mentioned him in one of our phone calls,' he explained. 'I rang the *Enquirer* and spoke to his secretary. She informed me that Mr Roach was on leave. When I said I'd try to contact him at home, she told me he was away, staying in a small pub in a village to the south of Warwick town.'

'And you thought we'd gone there for——'

'I didn't know why you'd gone,' Shafe interceded swiftly. 'What I did know was that Larry regards you as his protégée, his golden girl—and that somehow the big surprise didn't seem so wonderful any more. I spent my time in Paris convincing myself that there was a totally innocent explanation and that when I returned to London you'd be there to greet me. You weren't.'

Keri frowned. 'So you travelled on to New York thinking the worst?'

'I had peaks and troughs. One minute I was sure there was no way you'd do the dirty on me, the next——' He moved a hand. 'When I spoke to you on the phone I waited to be told about your trip, but you never said a goddamn word!'

'I was saving it.'

'Saving it?' Shafe asked quizzically.

'Yes.' She grinned. 'And I'm going to save it a few minutes longer—until you've finished talking.'

'Oh. OK.' He picked up the thread again. 'This lack of feedback woke me up to the fact that our relationship could be in danger of...disintegrating. Hell, for weeks I'd been expecting you to say you were coming back to New York, but it hadn't happened. Add Larry to the scenario and it was blue funk time. I decided no matter what nasties were unearthed, I must check things out person-to-person.'

'You were facing up to the demons again?' Keri suggested.

He gave a wry smile. 'I guess.'

'I was so surprised when you suggested a holiday in Barbados. Surprised and over the moon!'

'Were you? Jeez, we really had our wires crossed,' Shafe sighed. 'When I raised the idea there was a moment of silence—as though you didn't know what to say.'

'I didn't. I'd been struck dumb.'

'But I took it to mean you were reluctant. There was another pause when I spoke of sitting and talking, and straight away I attributed that to guilty feelings about your time in Warwickshire.'

'Our discussions were intended to clear the air as far as any affiliation with Larry was concerned,' Keri defined. 'That's all?'

'All! Honey, our marriage is the most important thing in my life. I'd go through fire and concrete walls to keep it intact.' He grinned, suddenly aware of his intensity. 'That wasn't necessary. I simply had to fix six weeks in Barbados. Though I had no idea those weeks would include filming a section of the Joseph Harewood profile.'

'It hadn't been previously arranged?'

'No. It was only when Bill Spiro learned of our destination that he muscled in and asked if I could manage a few days work.'

'So Emma and I did come first!' she said triumphantly.

'You...didn't think? You did.' Having answered his own question, Shafe reassembled his thoughts. 'Your reluctance to join me, as I imagined it, meant I arrived here determined to sweep you off your feet. I even hoped the moustache might dazzle you!' He made a face. 'But when we met at the airport, you gave the impression of being...aloof. That far, I'd been confident of halting any disintegration, then—then I began to wonder. Your hasty exit that night didn't help any. I'd told myself that if you were involved with Larry it must be lightweight stuff, but avoiding me seemed to point to you being in love with the guy!' He gave a hollow laugh. 'After that I panicked. It seemed the only way I could show how much I cared—and demonstrate my superiority to him, I guess—was to make love to you. I was determined that when we got into bed it would be the most cosmic event ever, but——' He closed his eyes. 'Did I ever mess up!'

Keri entwined her fingers with his. 'A high anxiety crisis. Not nice.'

'Bloody awful,' he said with feeling. 'Did you realise what had happened?'

'Not at first.'

'Doesn't surprise me. I could hardly believe it myself! There's a saying that when you want it bad, you get it bad. I did.' Shafe was silent for a moment. 'If you didn't know what had happened, why did you think I ... changed my mind?'

She attempted an offhand shrug. 'Allegiance to another woman. You do spend a lot of time away and——'

'Sleep in more bedrooms than Casanova? But I sleep in them alone.' A tanned hand was held up before her. 'Keri, see this golden band? It guarantees my allegiance to you and only you, now and for ever.' He kissed her. 'Understand?'

'I understand.'

'So, what were you doing in Warwickshire?'

'Working.'

Shafe gave a surprised laugh. 'But fifteen months ago you stopped being a career girl overnight. Since then the only pictures I've known you take have been of Emma.'

'Recently I've done others. Quite a lot, in fact. You see, devoted as I was, in time I had to admit that listening to a baby go glug, glug, glug, all day lacked stimulation. I also realised that if I didn't buck my ideas up there was a danger of me not only losing my identity, but also any chance of returning to photography in the future. So I experimented with a few shots, to check I was up to scratch, and——'

'This was in New York?'

'Yes. I was on the brink of phoning a couple of magazine contacts to remind them I still existed, when Angela rang to say Dad had been taken ill and could I fly over? Caring for him took up most of my day, but from time to time I'd wheel Emma off to a park and snap around. I managed to compile a modest portfolio and when Larry got in touch after my father died, I mentioned it. He'd always encouraged me in the past and——' Keri shrugged '—I hoped he would again. After lying dormant for so long, my confidence needed a boost.'

'And he did encourage you,' Shafe asserted.

She nodded. 'When he looked at the portfolio he bought a few of the shots there and then, for the files. He also said whatever else I did while I was in London, to show him. As Angela was wallowing in self-pity at the time, being active rather than stuck in the *re*active mode seemed essential if I was to keep sane, so I returned to photography with a vengeance. I moved from the park to river scenes: the Thames in all its moods, that kind of thing. Lugging Emma around as second mate had its problems, so——' she threw him a look '—a playgroup seemed ideal.'

'I thought you reckoned it was to provide *her* with an outlet!'

Keri grinned. 'Well——'

He gave a mock groan of despair. 'Where does Warwickshire come in?'

'Unknown to me, Larry had shown my portfolio to Robert, a friend from his schooldays. Robert's family were wealthy, and he'd inherited a manor house which dates back to the sixteenth century. Twice a week the house and gardens are open to the public, and he felt that a guide book would be useful, one with photographs of both interior and exterior. I was asked to take them.'

'But why did Larry go to Warwickshire with you?'

'Because Robert and his wife invited him. He had some leave due, which if he didn't take he'd lose, and as he hadn't had a break for almost twelve months, why not? He offered to take charge of Emma while I was otherwise engaged.' She chuckled. 'Larry claims to be a contented bachelor, but I suspect he could have been experimenting with how it feels to have a youngster around.'

'Did he like it?'

'On the whole, yes. Though he wasted no time in handing her back whenever she squawked.'

'You stayed together in the manor house?' Shafe asked.

'We did, Mr Interrogator. Larry occupied a room in the east wing, while Emma and I were a mile-long hike away over in the west.' She poked a finger in his ribs. 'Satisfied?'

'Yes, ma'am. Your photographs turn out OK?'

'Excellent, considering the outdoor ones had to be done in the rain. The guide book should be ready any time now. I'm not giving up my photography again,' she informed him. 'I can't work full-time and I don't want to, but I can do enough to keep a foot in the door.'

'Honey, I'm with you all the way.'

'Thanks.'

Shafe stroked the back of his fingers down her cheek. 'Thank you—for being you. And,' he added, his mouth curving, 'thank you for services rendered. I knew I'd recovered, but it sure felt great having it proved. I hate to harp back but, as a matter of interest, if you didn't cotton on straight away that I was——' he winced '—impotent, how long was it before you realised?'

'Less than a day. Although after that, though I felt sure, I was never cast-iron sure.' Keri smiled and fed his words back to him. 'As a matter of interest, how long did it take before you knew you'd recovered?'

'Less than a day. I woke up the next morning with——' he grinned 'I won't go into graphic detail. Hell, you know what I often wake up with. However, like you, although my cure seemed sure, I hesitated about being *too* sure. Tonight there was a split second when I wondered whether my biology might act against me, and everything would go kaput.'

'But it didn't.'

'And you won't let it. Keeping me sexually active is what you were referring to when we first started this conversation?' he asked, his eyes mischievous. 'Great,' Shafe said, when she nodded. 'It strikes me as supremely fitting for us to now end the conversation by finding out whether you were telling the truth or merely resorting to bravado?'

'We haven't ended the conversation.'

'No?'

'No.' She paused, biting the inside of her lip, then said in a rush, 'You may have come to Barbados to talk about Larry, but I came to talk about——'

'Toots, you never give up, do you?' Shafe murmured. He lifted the shiny curtain of blonde hair and brushed his lips across the warm skin behind her ear. 'Never. Never. Never.'

'Shafe, listen,' she protested, as he lifted his head and smiled. His gaze went to her mouth. She knew he was going to kiss her and she decided she wasn't going to kiss him back, but, of course, she did. 'Shafe,' she said again, when eventually they came up for air. 'About that newscasting job——'

He gave a soft chuckle. 'Honey, you're amazing!'

With his long fingers tracing erotic patterns across her breasts, Keri was having difficulty in speaking straight, let alone thinking straight.

'I'm serious,' she declared shakily.

'And when I said newscasting was not for me——' Shafe brushed his moustache back and forth across her collarbone '——I was serious, too.'

'You're being——'

'Cussed? No more so than you. Stop trying to ram the idea down my throat. I'm not going to change my mind.'

'Why not? It seems to me that——'

'Do you think you could observe one minute of silence? Please.'

Tenderly he kissed her brow, her chin, one high cheekbone and then the other.

'But——'

'Enough, Keri,' he murmured, and kissed her mouth.

She had no resistance left.

The patching of Emma's dungarees was almost complete before Keri realised she had been jabbing the needle through three layers of cloth, and had thus stitched up the trouser leg. With a sigh, she began the task of unpicking. After a night of love-making, she and Shafe had awakened to make love again. It had been wonderful. Everything was wonderful this morning, except... She re-threaded her needle. The newscasting job receiving a resounding raspberry for the *third* time had left them at what, for lack of a better description, she could only define as stalemate.

So where now? What next? When she returned with him to New York she would be putting her head back in the noose. Yet how could she not return? She loved him. She loved the stubborn, wilful man. Loved him to distraction. In, out, in, flew the needle. What did she do, grin and bear his absences? What else could she do? But she resented being strung up. Resented it deeply.

'Ouch!'

'Pricked your finger, toots?' Shafe sympathised, coming out on to the patio. He caught hold of her hand. 'Let me kiss it better. And if there's any other small thing you'd like me to kiss, I'm ready, willing and very able.'

'I'll try and think of something,' Keri promised.

'If you want to make an old man very happy, try hard. You have five minutes, while I go and buy a packet of cigars.' He looked out into the garden where Emma was wandering around, at a loose end because Suzette had taken the morning off to go to the dentist and Victor was not there to play. 'Fancy a ride in the moke, ragtag?'

The toddler did not need to be asked twice. The only pause in her bowlegged forward rush was a step which required to be negotiated, then she was demanding to be lifted up.

'Five minutes,' he repeated, with a farewell wave.

Left alone, Keri returned to her patching and her thoughts. She was trapped, frustratingly and maddeningly trapped, unless... Frowning, she recalled how her sister had taken it upon herself to form a 'war cabinet' of one. Not only had Angela dissected their marriage and identified failings, but she had also put forward suggestions guaranteed to make Shafe play patty cake. 'Walk out,' she had advocated in her hardline way. 'That'll bring him to his senses.' Keri grimaced. Of course, the action Angela would applaud most fervently would be if she walked out and kept on walking, and did it today. Her sister was a great gal for refusing to be trodden on. She would have had no truck with try, try, try again.

But Keri needed to try again. Somehow she had to get it through to him that her argument of their lives being so much richer if he became New York based made impeccable logic. She sighed. It could not be denied that so far all she had achieved from tackling Shafe head-on was a bruised head, so— did she walk out and give him that short, sharp shock? Could she steel herself to adopt such a tactic? For a nail-biting, heart-galloping moment, the needle hovered above the dungarees. If it represented the only way out of this rat's nest then, yes, she could and she would! Dire straits demanded dire actions. Keri plunged the needle into the cloth, then stopped. Such a fearsome event could not be rushed into. Shrewdly she must evaluate whether it was best to depart within the next few days, or if waiting a while would have more of an impact. She hated to be calculating—she hated, no *abhorred*, the idea of punishing Shafe like this—but she had reached the end of the road. Besides, hopefully just *telling* him she was going would do the trick. Please.

The crunch of tyres on the drive had Keri's galloping heart diving down. To plan a withdrawal when they were so in tune seemed sneaky, shabby, despicable. Every fibre of her being shouted out against it. If only it did not have to be so. Taking a deep breath, she ditched her mending and walked round to the front of the house. It was too distressing to think about her departure today. She would wait until tomorrow.

'Hello!' she said, surprised to find Baz Guiler climbing out of a shiny red moke.

He greeted her, then lifted a large, and what looked to be heavy, cardboard box from the back seat.

'This is for your little girl. It's to make amends for losing my temper the other morning. For feeding you a crock of utter——' he substituted a word for the one he had chosen '—rubbish. And for being drunk. Very drunk.'

'Oh, thank you. Shafe's taken Emma out, but they shouldn't be more than a few minutes. Perhaps you'd like to wait?'

'Will do.' Baz tightened his hold on the box and followed her to the patio. 'Rise to a kingpin position like I've done,' he said, jettisoning his load and taking possession of a chair, 'and the hangers-on tell you what you want to hear, not what you need to hear. When you accused me of swilling down the booze, you were right and I knew you were right—though it took me a while to accept it. However,' her visitor announced proudly, 'I've been on the wagon for the past week.'

'Does that mean I'm not allowed to offer you a drink?'

'I could accept a Coke, if you twisted my arm.'

'Has staying on the wagon been purgatory?' Keri enquired, when she returned from the kitchen with two glasses, each clinking with ice.

Baz shuddered. 'Purgatory isn't the word. But don't let's discuss the bad times, let's stick to the good. Tell me about your holiday.'

She grinned. 'Ten days ago I was rushed into hospital to have my appendix removed.'

'And here I am, grumbling!' He slapped a palm to his brow. 'Sorry to hear you've been through it, flower. How are you feeling now?'

'Fully recovered.'

Baz asked about the hospital and her convalescence, then returned to the reason for his visit.

'I owe you an apology for my spiel. To be honest, it's become a standard production whenever I'm feeling down. I was down that morning. I'd received a letter from the drummer in my old group and in it was a mention of Jo.' He drank a mouthful of Coke. 'It's stupid me caring so much after all this time, but it's something I have to live with. Something no amount of alcohol will change. Seems she's a travel courier now,' he continued, more cheerfully. 'It's the ideal job for her; she always did have a thing about living on the hoof.'

'Sounds like my husband.'

'What does he do?'

Keri explained and because, once again, Baz was a good listener, at greater length than intended. Shafe's life-style was described, plus his rejection of the newscasting job.

'Over the years he's clocked up quite a mileage,' she concluded, then could not resist adding, 'but all good things must come to an end.'

'He's going to pack in reporting?'

Determination entered her voice. 'He is.'

'Why?'

'Why?' she repeated, amazed such a question needed to be asked. 'Because Emma and I deserve some consideration, that's why!'

'Does *he* want to pack it in?' Baz enquired.

'Shafe'll see the advantages.'

'Advantages for him or advantages for you? Flower, I don't know what's going off between you and your husband, and it's none of my business, but I'd advise you to think carefully about what it is you want from life.'

'I know what I want,' Keri replied firmly.

'Do you? I wonder.' Baz put his glass aside. 'The reason Jocasta and I split was because I made the mistake you seem to be making—I was trying to impose my will.'

A shadow crossed her face. His description might be apt, but it disturbed her. 'For the full two years we've been married, Shafe has come and gone to suit himself,' she said defensively. 'Isn't it only fair that now——'

'Now he strays no further than a fifty-mile radius? That'd be for two years, then it'd be all change again, would it?'

'Well...no,' Keri faltered.

'If you're talking about fairness a two-year slug of what suits him, followed by two years of what suits you, must then be followed by two years of——'

'That wouldn't be practical.'

'No, from all points of view. I imagine if your husband quits news reporting, he'd find it well nigh impossible to return. Though you don't intend him to return, do you? You intend to brainwash him into believing he's better off without a job which, for years, has kept him happy and stimulated.'

'Brainwashing doesn't come into this,' she said, beginning to find the conversation irksome.

Baz's reply was a wry smile. 'Let me tell you about me and Jo, then you'll understand what I'm getting at.'

Keri reached for the dungarees. Her visitor was too fond of the sound of his own voice, she thought uncharitably. She had no interest in what he might be 'getting at'. All that interested her was Shafe and Emma returning and putting an end to a discussion she wished she had never started. For him to find a similarity between his affair with a teeny-bopper and her marriage was farcical!

'Jo, like your husband, owned a pair of itchy feet,' Baz began, with the dedicated air of a story-teller. 'Six months after we first met, she woke up one morning and announced she'd been in one place too long. I had a tour of the States lined up, so I said if she wanted to travel then travelling with me through America would be as good as she could get.' He leant forward to shake an admonishing finger. 'Not on your life! Jo intended to take off to see some Turkish ruins. I couldn't understand it. There was I, offering first-class flights, luxury hotels, the chance to wine and dine in style, and she was pining for wandering barren hills and eating cold stew out of a billycan!'

'Did she go on the tour?' Keri asked, drawn in against her will.

'After I'd argued and coaxed and pleaded, yeah. I even had my agent tell her I wouldn't be able to perform at my best unless she came along! I was going to have her there if it killed me. And for the entire tour. Got a bee in my bonnet, y'see. Never thought of her going to Turkey first and coming on to join me. Or any other alternative where she'd give a little, I'd give a little, and we'd meet halfway. 'Course, we'd barely set foot back in England before she hopped off to Ankara without telling me—to save any fuss. In the year which followed, the wanderlust struck her a couple more times and on each occasion I made my resentment plain.' Baz heaved a sigh. 'The last time she went, she stayed away for ever.'

'But you can't equate your experiences with mine, or Jo with Shafe,' Keri protested. 'Her absences were short. Besides, she wasn't married to you. She didn't have a child waiting at home.'

'Her absences weren't work-induced absences, either. She wasn't consolidating her career, wasn't committed to a network, wasn't involved in bringing home the bacon.'

'Shafe could bring home the bacon if he *was* at home.'

'He must be a newscaster or nothing, that's the choice you're giving him?'

Keri pouted. Admitting to a single train of thought seemed feeble.

'What if he says no?' her visitor demanded. 'Or has he already said it?'

'Shafe isn't in favour,' she admitted, squirming beneath Baz's glance.

'What's your next step, flower—walking out?'

Her cheeks burned. Was this a random guess, or had he detected something in her manner? Whatever, hearing her plan depicted in words was not pleasant, not pleasant at all.

'Er——'

'Let's imagine your husband refuses to comply even then, where does that leave you—suing for divorce?'

Keri choked on the idea. 'Er——' was all she could manage again.

'On the other hand, suppose he submits to your blackmail, then spends the rest of his life aware of something lacking. Is that going to make you happy?'

'Reminding him of his loyalty towards me and Emma is not blackmail,' she retorted, unable to answer the charge of Shafe missing out or how she would feel about it.

'Maybe, maybe not. But shouldn't you consider a compromise?'

Her chin jutted. 'Shafe should compromise.'

'By opting for newscasting? You call it a compromise, others might describe it as capitulation.' Baz folded tattooed forearms. 'I agree when a man marries he makes a commitment, and included in that commitment is him being around a fair part of the time. Fair as in fair play. Fair as in mutual agreement.'

'There's been no agreement!'

'Flower, by accepting the situation from the start you've agreed. Sorry, but that's how it goes. How many months of the year is your husband away?'

'I've never worked it out in total.' Keri screwed up her face. 'About six.'

'For how long a period?'

'Depends where the news is. Sometimes four or five days but, if he flies from one country to the next direct, occasionally ten.'

'Could be worse.'

'I suppose so,' she mumbled.

For a quarter of an hour Keri had been aware of doubts stealthily creeping up behind, but now they had placed their claws on her shoulders. As Baz had had 'a bee in his bonnet' as he had described it, so, it seemed, had she. Why the obsession with the newscasting job? Why had she demanded Shafe give a knee-jerk affirmative to something she knew would never capture his full interest? Why, in all her plans, had no margin of flexibility been allowed? The doubts gripped hard and shook her. Why had she never considered occasionally joining Shafe on his travels? What had happened to collaboration? Why had she ignored the middle ground—as Angela always did?

Fastening off the thread, Keri set the dungarees aside. Throughout four months of cheek-by-jowl living, scarcely a week had gone by without her sister depicting a relationship where Shafe featured as villain, while Keri had been the innocently wronged spouse. When bombarded like that, always her scorn had been total, her rejection absolute, and yet... Could Angela's ideas have been subconsciously absorbed? Had some of her intolerance rubbed off? In New York, although Keri had not welcomed Shafe's absences, she had taken them in her stride and suffered no sense of impoverishment. Yet in London she had come to regard herself as unjustly discarded. She had believed him 'never there'; though her assessment of Shafe living at home fifty per cent of the year said otherwise.

Now it was clear that her memories of the past had become distorted. Keri shuddered, thinking how she had been prepared to use walking out as a mallet to pound Shafe into the newscasting slot. What a muddle-headed, narrow-minded over-reaction! And reckless to the extent of kamikaze! She looked across at Baz and gave up heartfelt thanks for his well-timed arrival and his common sense.

'I do seem to have mislaid my sense of balance,' Keri admitted, with an embarrassed smile. 'You're right, I should think in terms of a compromise.'

The rock star grinned. 'That's it. Be smart.' Hearing the sound of a car, he tilted his head. 'Sounds like your family's returned.'

Seconds later, Shafe and Emma appeared around the corner of the patio.

'Why the delay?' Keri enquired, when everyone had been introduced.

'The woman in the shop made a fuss over ragtag here, then her sister-in-law arrived and, after that, what seemed like half the village.' He grinned. 'If I'd had any sense I'd have taken Emma with me on my travels long ago. She opens more doors in two minutes than I can manage in a week!'

'I understand you report the news on an international basis,' the older man remarked. 'Sounds fascinating.'

'It is.'

'Functioning as a loner professionally must depend upon having the back-up of a secure home life?'

Shafe's eyes narrowed. Despite Keri's comments, he had dismissed Baz Guiler as a blockhead of paltry interest, but the astute observation demanded a reappraisal.

'I guess it does,' he replied guardedly. He looked about to say more, but spying the cardboard box, Emma had gone to investigate and was beating a tattoo on the side. 'Go easy, ragtag,' he called.

'That's OK. It's for her and it won't hurt,' Baz assured him. 'You ought to know that I'm here to apologise for being the worse for wear the other morning and——' he grinned '—that as I'm the kind of low individual who'll try to buy his way back into favour, I've brought a peace offering.'

Shafe gave a half-hearted smile, uncertain whether he should approve.

'Want to see Mr Guiler's present, Emma?' Keri asked, determined to avoid an awkward hiatus.

'Shall I open it, petal?' their visitor asked. He walked over to crouch down beside the little girl. 'And forget all this jazz about Mr Guiler, the name's Baz.'

As suspicious as her father, Emma gave the smiling face a doubtful scrutiny. Finally she smiled, too.

'Gaga!' she exclaimed.

A shared glance left Shafe grinning, while Keri needed to bite her lip. Both of their fathers had been delighted to be christened 'Gaga', though whether Baz, in his too-tight jeans and trendy white silk shirt, would appreciate being identified as a grandfather was a different matter.

'Yes, Baz,' he crowed, obligingly taking the name as a version of his own. He ripped securing tape from the box and, as Emma leaned precariously in, removed wads of foam. 'Suit you, petal?' he enquired, producing a shiny red, white and blue pedal car.

'Suit her?' Shafe exclaimed, coming over for a closer inspection. 'It's magnificent! If she doesn't hurry up and climb aboard, I'll be in there driving it myself.'

But Emma was cautious. She looked at the car. In time, she ventured out chubby fingers and touched the car. She almost agreed to be lifted *into* the car, then changed her mind.

'Maamee,' she muttered, pushing her head against Keri's knee.

'You sit on the seat, put your feet on the pedals and push,' Baz coaxed.

'It'll be fun,' Shafe encouraged.

When his daughter remained dubious he steered the car around, to the accompaniment of Baz's running commentary.

'The lines of this remind me of an old MG I had once,' their visitor said, as the toddler continued to shilly-shally.

Shafe straightened. 'I've always hankered after an MG myself. Which model did you have?'

When Emma did agree to make friends with her gift, it was Keri who lifted her in, because the two men were deep into a discussion of acceleration, noise levels and gas consumption. But they did take notice when, by dint of haphazard pedalling, Emma managed to propel herself a yard or two.

'Clever girl!' exclaimed Baz, and grinned at Shafe. 'You've got a smart kid there.'

He smiled. 'I know it.'

'And a smart wife. Look after them both.'

For a moment Shafe's features tightened as though the remark had unleashed myriad thoughts. 'Don't worry, I will,' he replied, with infinite precision.

'About the interview with the *Enquirer*,' Baz said, turning to Keri. 'Would you tell that Roach guy I'll do it?'

'You will? Are you sure?' she asked, wondering if the morning's companionship could be prompting an offer which might later be regretted and retracted. 'To be frank, it makes no difference to me whether——'

'The interview could make a difference to *me*. I intended to mention it earlier, but——' he slid her a wink '—we became involved in another subject. The point is, some publicity could come in useful.'

'How?' Shafe enquired.

Baz blew out a breath. 'To explain that I need to explain that writing a musical has long been one of my ambitions. Before I came to Barbados I'd already thought out a plot, identified where songs were needed, and as soon as I moved into the bungalow I started work. After two or three months of intense productivity, I regret to say the drinking took over. End of musical. However, this week I've been reading through what I'd done and——' pride swelled his chest '—it's obvious I'm sitting on a winner. The minute I finish the score I'll be out there touting for backers, and attracting them'll be that much easier if my name's fresh in their minds.'

'It also wouldn't hurt to give backers, and the general public, advance warning of what you're doing,' Shafe suggested.

'Whet the appetites by mentioning the musical? Good idea.'

'You wouldn't be interested in some exposure on television in the States?' Shafe asked, with what Keri recognised as fake indolence. He did not waste his time on useless queries. They always had a purpose.

Baz pursed his lips, considering. 'Depends on who did the interview.'

'Me?'

'Then I'd agree.'

'I'd better tell you here and now, I'm not into soft ball. On occasions, I hit hard.'

Again the rock star took time to consider. 'You'd want to air the question of my drinking? What caused it? That kind of thing?'

'I can't say until I've thought an interview through, but it's a possibility,' Shafe warned him.

'I'll do it,' Baz decided. 'When do we start?'

'Hold it a minute,' Shafe protested, 'we can't start anything without I have the network's approval.'

'Why not ring Bill Spiro now?' Keri intervened eagerly. 'And as a crew'll already be in Barbados for Joey's profile, you could suggest they stay on and film Baz.'

He looked pensive. 'Honey, we're here for a vacation. Though I guess we could extend,' he agreed.

'So go on, call Bill. If he's interested, then at least Baz'll know where he stands.'

She received another pensive glance. 'Yes, ma'am.'

The approach of noon was causing the mercury to soar, and as Shafe disappeared Keri went to fix fresh drinks. When she returned she found Baz, sweat streaming down his face, propelling Emma around the garden. The patio, it transpired, had become a snap and the lawn had beckoned. Attempting to trundle across thick-bladed grass beneath the glare of the tropical sun could not be rated the wisest of moves, but with her assistant's help the toddler achieved a fair degree of momentum.

'Shafe's still speaking to New York,' Keri apologised ten minutes later when the patio had returned to favour and Baz hauled both car and driver back on to the marble.

'No—no hurry,' he puffed, now involved in pushing Emma from one side to the other.

Why should the call take such a long time? Keri wondered. What made it so involved? With the telephone positioned in an alcove off the living-room it was impossible to decipher more than an odd word, yet she could hear enough to know Shafe was switching around between argument, discussions and persuasion. Could it be that although she considered Baz box office, Bill Spiro regarded him a back number? Or was the rock star's past, which the moral majority could rightly claim had been exemplary bad living, the reason for hesitation? Bill would not risk a drop in ratings by causing offence. She strained to hear, but without success. Maybe Shafe's problem was not getting USB to accept Baz Guiler, but getting them to accept *him* as interviewer? The Joey profile was a one-off, and his forte was the news, not personalities.

Another quarter of an hour passed by before Shafe replaced the receiver. Keri awaited his approach with apprehension, but he returned to the patio with his eyes shining and a spring in his step.

'Bill likes the idea, likes it very much. A letter stating terms, et cetera, should reach you within the next few days, Baz, so if everything suits give me a ring and we'll take it from there.'

The older man nodded agreement. He had straightened up to receive the verdict, but now he bent to rumple Emma's curls. 'Sorry to leave you, petal, but it's time to say goodbye. I promised myself at least four hours' hard writing in each twenty-four and I'm way behind schedule.'

'We're shooting the last portion of Joseph Harewood's profile aboard the *Bajan Buccaneer* in around three weeks' time. Why not join us?' Shafe suggested, as Baz climbed into his moke. 'It'd give you a chance to see how I work.'

Their visitor laughed. 'You mean, it'd give me a chance to see how much blood you leave on the deck?'

'No blood, just guts,' he grinned. ''Bye.'

''Bye,' said Keri.

''Bye, gaga,' trilled Emma.

'Y'know, Guiler isn't such a bad guy, after all,' Shafe remarked, as Baz sped away and they walked back to the patio.

'But Bill Spiro thought he was, at first? He argued a case against him?'

'Nope. The profile was fixed in minutes,' he replied, lifting an enthusiastic Emma back into her car.

Keri gave him a querying look. 'Then why were you on the phone all that time?'

Shafe placed his hands on her upper arms and steered her down on to the settee. That done, he pulled up a chair and faced her. Serious grey eyes met hers.

'Because I needed to speak to Bill about my long-term career.'

'What about it?' she asked cautiously.

'Honey, ever since we arrived here you've been putting forward a strong case for me accepting that newscaster's job and staying at home. At first, I admit I thought you were crazy, but things have happened which have altered my perspective and now——'

'No!' Keri's hand flew to her throat in panic. 'I was wrong! You can't take on something as deadly as reading the news! I won't let you! Shafe, you *mustn't*!'

CHAPTER EIGHT

'KERI, listen—'

'Nothing definite's been agreed, has it? It can't! And even if Mr Spiro has given you the job you haven't signed on the dotted line, so it must be reversible. Call him back. Do it now.' The words were tumbling out. 'Tell him you've changed your mind. OK, he'll shout and swear and accuse you of being all kinds of things, including stupid, but I'm the one who's been stupid,' she said chokily. 'Me.'

Shafe moved from his chair to sit beside her.

'Honey, you're not stupid,' he said, enclosing her in his arms.

'I am! I have been. I should have known it's not the amount of time we spend together that matters, but the quality. Oh, Shafe, all those months in London, with Angela being so...so picky, somehow influenced me. I decided your travelling was too much to take, and fastened on to you becoming a newscaster.' Keri brushed a hand across her eyes. 'I polished and polished until the idea shone so brightly it blinded me to anything else. Like *your* feelings.'

He pressed his lips to her brow.

'Don't cry.'

'I'm not. Yes, I am,' she agreed, gazing up through a blur of tears. 'I convinced myself that newscasting was the be-all and end-all, but I was wrong.'

Shafe gave a lopsided smile. 'You've decided you couldn't stand me perpetually under your feet?'

'It isn't a question of that. It's a question of us pulling together, being a team,' she said, too wound up to take his remark as anything less than deadly serious. 'Shafe, newscasting would be a disaster.'

'I agree.'

Her eyes opened wide. 'You—you do?' she stuttered.

'Yep.' He kissed away the tear which had rolled down her cheek. 'Which is why I never raised the idea with Bill.'

There was silence. The discovery that she had been pleading with him not to take a job he had never even considered left Keri floundering.

'So what idea *did* you raise?' she enquired.

'Me broadening my base.'

Her heart sank. Base-broadening sounded horribly like an increase in his trips to distant places, a lengthening of his absences. But her interpretation of them pulling together required Shafe's current home occupancy rate to be maintained, not diminished.

'Which means?' Keri asked, experiencing a violent attack of the collywobbles.

'Quitting news reporting and concentrating on profiles, documentaries and in-depth political reviews. Which also means that instead of my home-away ratio being around fifty-fifty, it'll be more like seventy-thirty.' Shafe was watching her with anxious eyes. 'Think you can live with that?'

'Live with it?' Such a declaration should have been accompanied by a drum roll, if not fireworks exploding in mid-air. She clasped her hands around the back of his neck and gave a brilliant smile. 'Yes,

I can live with it.' Her smile dimmed a watt or two. 'But can you?'

'Of course.'

'It's not of course,' Keri protested. 'Reporting is what gives you your kicks.'

'In the days when I was single, yes. Now?' Shafe shook his head. 'It's been a gradual process, but much of the thrill has gone. Now reporting has too many drawbacks.'

'Like?'

'Like I have a horror of a white knight appearing while I'm in distant lands and galloping off with my lady. Like I'm fed up with being so damn celibate I could give lessons to monks.' He looked beyond her and grinned. 'Like I want to be around to watch Ayrton Senna, who's in danger of falling asleep at the wheel, grow up.'

Sucking solidly at her thumb, Emma allowed him to lift her out of the pedal car. A nap seemed definite, until Keri went into the kitchen to make lunch. Then memories of yesterday's dessert had the cornflower-blue eyes opening wide and a hand pointing towards her high chair.

'Was the profile on Joey Bill Spiro's brainchild?' Keri asked, as their daughter ate a last mouthful of minced beef and ogled a newly delivered bowl of mango ice-cream.

'No, it was mine. After being steeped in reporting for six or seven years now, the prospect of giving up wasn't that easy to get used to and for a long while I ... hedged. However, even though my feelings were in a state of flux, it did seem sensible to locate a viable alternative and I decided to experiment. Profiles had a lot going for them because, for a start, they meant I wouldn't be flying off here, there and everywhere at a moment's notice. And, when I did fly, to a large extent the timing would be under my control, which would make it easier to meld in with our home life.'

'Also the contacts you've made over the years will ensure you'll never run short of subjects,' Keri put in.

'It wasn't your brain which first attracted me, but I sure appreciate you having one,' Shafe replied drily. He lurched back. 'Don't hit me!'

She thrust a fist under his chin. 'Then apologise.'

'I do. I do. You have brains, beauty, and the skin at the top of your thighs is so silky-smooth it could drive a man insane. As it almost did last night. And this morning. And, if you have any pity, will again, real soon.' He gave a theatrical groan. 'Please.'

'I'll consider it,' Keri said, laughing. She spent a minute or two persuading Emma that eating ice-cream with a spoon scored over scooping it in with fingers, then asked, 'Why did you choose Joseph Harewood for the profile? Why not one of your politicians?'

'Joey was symbolic. He brought us together in the first place and so, as you and I were——' Shafe waggled a hand '—shaky, renewing contact with the guy seemed like we had a better chance of getting *back* together. There was no logic involved, just lots of emotion, but that's how I felt. Explaining what made him special to an abrasive tough-nut like Bill was impossible, so——' he rolled despairing eyes '—did I ever have a problem convincing him Joey was my man!'

She grinned. 'He thought you'd taken leave of your senses?'

'A certified nut. I had to work on him for ages, and when he did give the go-ahead I'm convinced it was only to humour me. But Joey's a TV natural, so after Bill'd seen the initial footage he moseyed along to my office and confessed my suggestion hadn't been as kooky as he'd imagined.' He smiled at Emma's clean bowl, sticky face, messy T-shirt. 'Someone's enjoyed their ice-cream. And that someone's tired,' he added, as a thumb found its way to a mouth.

The toddler slumped while Keri was washing her, closed her eyes as her clothes were being changed, and in seconds was fast asleep.

'All on our own,' Shafe said contentedly, when Keri returned to the living-room. He entwined his fingers with hers and pulled her close. 'You're the one with the brains, toots. Got any ideas as to how——' he lifted his eyebrows '——we could profitably pass the next hour or two?'

'Well, Suzette won't be in until four and——'

'Yes?' he prompted eagerly. 'Yes?'

'And it seems mean to expect her to arrive and find a stack of dirty dishes, so how about us doing them for her?'

His reply was an expletive.

Together they cleared the table then, as Shafe armed himself with a tea towel, Keri began the washing up.

'If Joey's profile was only done as an experiment, then it follows that somewhere along the line your views have firmed up, and drastically,' she said. 'I presume this firming-up is recent?'

'Very recent. Mind you, although I've only just seen the light, it has been flickering—if uncertainly.' Slowly he circled the cloth over a plate.

'What I was certain of when I touched down in Barbardos was: one, we were growing apart and I didn't like it; two, I missed you like hell; three, if there was to be a duel with Larry Roach, I'd fight to the death. That little trio occupied me to such an extent that when you zapped me with your newscasting ideas they seemed...irrelevant. I would have been prepared to discuss my career, but in my own time. However, there was no time because the next minute I was impotent, the one after that you were on the operating table, and—boom!—I'd been left in sole charge of a one-year-old.'

'Some people have all the luck,' Keri commented wryly.

'Being forced to look after Emma for what seemed like forty-eight hours a day was the best thing which could have happened,' Shafe affirmed. 'It may have been a baptism of fire, but it brought the two of us close in double quick time. Not only that, it made me face up to the reality of how it feels to bring up a child on your own.' He stacked the plate away in a cupboard and turned to her. 'As you'd been doing, not only for the past four months, but for a year previously.'

Keri shook her head, determined to be fair. 'For six months out of that year.'

'Six months is still one hell of a long time. Too long.'

'Has the nappy-and-sticky-fingers syndrome been getting to you?' she asked lightly.

'No.'

'No?' she repeated in flagrant disbelief.

'No,' Shafe said, his voice firm. 'Honey, I know that ever since you came out of hospital you've been waiting for me to crack and run amok, screaming that looking after Emma is sheer drudgery and not for me, but you're mistaken. What I found so hard to handle that night when she cut up rough was being responsible for the safety of another human being. I mean it,' he insisted, when she frowned. 'I've occupied some pretty tight corners in my time, but nothing approaches the terror I felt then. I know she wasn't in any danger or, at least, I know it *now*. But at the time—oh, boy!'

Keri washed a last glass and tipped the water away. 'Your dialogue at the hospital did hint you could be feeling a certain strain,' she grinned, happy in the realisation that Shafe's days of 'playing at daddies' had been replaced by sturdy commitment. 'Strange,' she kidded, 'when the previous evening you'd been eulogising.'

'But that's how it goes, isn't it?' he said, ignoring her teasing. 'Be with a kid on a one-to-one basis and it's difficult to avoid them taking you over—actions, thoughts, conversation.' The drying complete, he hung the tea towel on the rail. 'Now I understand how Emma filled your life in New York. If I'd been in that situation, I figure I'd have reacted in just the same way.'

Keri gave half a smile, half a grimace. 'You'd have gone over the top?'

'If you did, it's understandable. Hell, all the time I was away you'd been storing up events, so it was natural that when I came home you should want to talk about them. Yet I got so bloody irritated!' Shafe came and put his arms around her. 'I love you, Keri,' he said huskily. 'I want to share your life, and I want to be fully involved in bringing up our child.' He kissed her lips. 'And, in time, our children.'

She smiled into his eyes, such soft grey eyes.

'So we should thank Miss Emma Rokeby for your illumination?'

'She did her bit, though the finger which finally flicked the switch belonged to Baz. The connection he made earlier between a secure home life and being able to work as a loner professionally hit me——' he punched a fist against his chest '—right there. I realised that wherever I was, north, south, east or west, I derived immeasurable comfort from simply knowing you were waiting for me, loving me. What's more, that comfort was vital. I needed it in order to function. I depended on it.'

'Before we were married you functioned well enough,' she pointed out.

'Only because I didn't know what I was missing. Baz's instruction to look after you and Emma crystallised everything. It was like he was warning me to wise up. I did! In a flash, any uncertainties vanished. I knew what I wanted and what I must do to get it.' Shafe smiled. 'It seems odd I should've been taught that "us" is the most important word in my vocabulary by a loose-living character who's never been married.'

'Baz is capable of making an awful lot of sense at times,' Keri acknowledged happily. She paused. 'Bill Spiro won't change his mind about you taking off in this new direction?'

Shafe shook his head. 'Having seen the majority of the Joey profile he reckons he is, as Baz would modestly claim, sitting on a winner. This being so, he's commissioned me to do four more in addition to the one on Guiler. And that's only for starters.'

'Then what was the arguing about?'

'Time scale. I told him I wanted to switch to profiles as soon as I returned to work, but Bill ob-
jected. He argued that it'd be better if I eased my
way out of reporting over a matter of months.'

'Better from the point of view of your career?'
she queried.

'Better from the point of view of him being able
to play God by holding endless meetings and
keeping everyone on edge while my replacement is
slowly-slowly selected!' Shafe scoffed.

'You got your way in the end?'

'Yup. Bill enjoys a power struggle—we had a hell
of an argument before he'd agree to me taking six
weeks' leave—but he's well aware other networks
will be quick off the mark if I show signs of becoming disenchanted.' The arms around her
tightened. 'Speaking of disenchantment, I'm fed
up to the back teeth with all this talking. How's
about we go and lie down and make no noise at
all?'

'Not even the occasional gasp?' Keri asked, as
he led her into the bedroom.

'A gasp is permissible,' he smiled, his eyes full
of loving lights. 'And now, Mrs Rokeby, I'm about
to undress you, so—quiet!'

Was it the silence, Keri wondered dreamily, which
made her body more aware of his than it had ever
been before, which made his mouth so tenderly seductive, which gave his touch that thrill? By the
time she was naked, she was trembling with anticipation and desire. Shafe stripped off his own clothes
and came to her on the bed. When she put her hands
on his shoulders his skin was warm and smooth. It
begged to be tasted. She rubbed her mouth against
the firm muscles, parting her lips to give moist,

teasing kisses as she rejoiced in his clean male fragrance. Her mouth moved lower, across the furze of tawny hair which covered his chest. She stroked her tongue over his nipples, ran her hand down and down until she felt the throbbing heat of his arousal.

'I never thought I'd be the one who gasped first,' he said shakily.

'Hush.'

Breathing hard, Shafe lay there submitting to the sweet torture until the moment came when he could stand it no longer and he entwined his hands into the rich curtain of her hair. He brought her up until their eyes and mouths were level, their bodies pressed together. They kissed, the urgency growing until, by instinct, they drew back and gazed at each other. No words were needed. Both knew that this was sharing. This was involvement. This was true love.

As his body covered hers, Keri wound her arms around him. She was lit up from inside. From outside. She glowed. Eyes closed, she writhed against him. A wave of sensation struck, weakened, left her gasping. She gasped again as Shafe began to move, slowly at first then faster, faster, faster. The wave struck a second time, but now he gripped her tight, carrying her with him, forcing her along on a high, high crest until he muttered something unintelligible against her mouth and they plunged— whirling, slewing, drowning together in a delirious sea.

'When I think of how we've been apart for the past two long, pointless months, I want to weep,' Shafe proclaimed, as he stepped out of the shower. He reached for a towel. 'Maybe caveman tactics are out of date, but how I wish I'd had the wit to grab you by the hair and drag you home—and to hell with putting your father's affairs in order or playing nursemaid to Angela! Instead I pussyfooted around, waiting——'

'That was the trouble, you waited,' Keri cut in. 'I didn't want waiting. I wanted complaints, frustration, to be told how miserable you were without me.'

'I was!'

'You didn't sound it. You sounded so...independent. Every time you phoned I thought, today he'll tell me the agonies he's going through, today he'll beg me to come back to New York. And I would have done.'

'Then what stopped you? There was more than me being stoical, Keri. There was you at the other end of the line making excuses and holding back,' he rebuked. 'Even if Angela did cause a delay, there was no reason why you couldn't have returned once she was fit.'

'No, but——' In preparation for the beach, she was wearing a bikini with one of Shafe's shirts as a coverall, and she began rolling up the sleeve. 'There were so many buts. But I longed to be told how desperately you needed me. But I wanted to punish you because you *didn't* tell me.' Keri sighed. 'That sounds petty-minded now, yet at the time, with Angela exhorting assertiveness and feminist rights and heaven knows what, it seemed reasonable. But I wanted you to become a newscaster, yet I couldn't get comfortable with the idea of demanding you accept a job you'd already turned down. But I hankered after some photographic

success because that would make me feel less of a
brood mare and more...with-it.'

Shafe dumped the towel. 'Honey, brood mares
don't come equipped with quick wits, high breasts
and slim hips. And mile-long legs.'

She leaned against him. 'Sure?'

'Positive. And as far as being with-it goes, you
never have been, and never will be, without it. And,'
he informed her seriously, 'I'm positive about that,
too.'

Keri sat on the lower deck of the *Bajan Buccaneer*,
bouncing her daughter up and down on her knee.
'Ride a Cock Horse' had been nominated as game
of the day, and the moment one cycle ended,
Emma, who had entered a particularly giggly stage,
demanded more. Laughing, Keri complied. It was
shady here and quiet, the only noise an occasional
creak of timbers or a flap-flap as the breeze tugged
and twitched at the huge red sails.

'Good to know someone's got sense,' commented a dark-skinned sailor as he ambled past.
Like the rest of the crew, he wore a pirate's outfit
of blue, full-sleeved shirt and breeches, with a white
bandanna knotted around his head. He pointed
towards the top deck. 'They're packed tight as sar-
dines up there and for what? To watch two guys
talking!'

Keri grinned. By declaring himself singularly unimpressed, the man was in the minority. Most of
the other people on board were fascinated. The rush
when the interview had shown signs of starting had
been lemming-like. One moment there had been
space aplenty in the bows, the next crowds were in
situ. The area roped off to accommodate partici-

pants and camera had remained inviolate, but every other inch of space was filled. On top deck at the time, Keri had been wondering whether to stay or go—how much sun could Emma take?—until the jostling had made the decision for her.

'Mind if I give this a miss?' she had asked Shafe.

Eyeing the crowds, he had grimaced. 'Go ahead. I'd give it a miss myself if I could.'

Although quiet, the past hour had been full of interest. As the schooner had sailed up the coast Keri had picked out a creek they had visited, a beachside inn where they had stopped for drinks, the landscaped gardens of a chic resort where they had spent a fortune on an intimate dinner for two. She planned to show Shafe these landmarks on the return journey.

From time to time Keri had made brief trips to the upper deck to check on progress. First, action had been delayed due to the microphone picking up extraneous noise, then a five-minute wait had been necessary to allow a rogue cloud, the only one in a sky of unrelenting blue, to pass by. After that the camera had rolled. About to start into 'Ride a Cock Horse' for what seemed like the twentieth time, Keri hesitated as a round of applause and cheers rang out from above.

'Daddy's finished,' she told Emma, and scooped her up. 'Suppose we go and say hello?'

An easy remark, a simple suggestion, yet when she had clambered up the companion way it was to find that others had had the same idea. Encircled by holidaymakers, Shafe was shaking hands, signing his name, and dealing with a hundred and one questions. When he saw the pair of them, he grinned.

'I'll be with you as quick as I can,' he mouthed.

Keri nodded and was on the point of retreat, when Baz forestalled her. His eagerness to give her an update of his activities meant that fast on the heels of the saga of his religious avoidance of the bottle came a detailed account of how his musical was shaping up. For the first ten minutes she listened, but after that Keri's true interest centred on whether the group around Shafe would ever thin. Baz's recital was curtailed when an adoring teenager asked for his autograph, but immediately his place was taken by Joseph Harewood, a stocky figure in lemon shirt and batik shorts. They had met earlier, but their contact had been brief, and now the businessman wanted to consolidate.

'Great to see ya again, kiddo,' he grinned.

Keri flashed a final hopeful glance and, finding Shafe as busy as before, gave Joey her full attention. Emma needed to be properly introduced, his wife called over to coo and admire, and subsequently catching up on two years' worth of news took time. She was laughing at one of Joey's comments, when a malty voice whispered in her ear.

'There's something about blonde, windswept hair hanging down a suntanned back which I find immensely erotic.' Shafe slipped an arm around her shoulders. 'Hi, toots.'

She smiled up at him. 'Hi.'

Joey beamed, relishing the interplay. 'So you two are as pie-eyed about each other as ever—that's great.' He cupped his ear, responding to a loud splash. 'Sounds like that was the anchor, and if we're mooring up it can only mean lunch. That's great, too.' He patted his ample girth. 'Being interviewed makes a guy hungry.'

This final questioning, so Shafe told her as they collected sizzling steaks and chose from the salad bar, put the seal on a programme which, in his view and Bill Spiro's, contained the ingredients essential for interesting, informative and stimulating television.

'Think you can coax more of the same from Baz?' Keri enquired.

'Watch me!'

After lunch there was a lull for drinking coffee and chatting, and later they sailed off in a glass-bottomed boat to inspect the coral, while more sportive individuals snorkelled or dived or learned how to jet-ski. On their return, Shafe and Keri swam while Baz kindly babysat, and then the *Bajan Buccaneer* set sail again. A steel band had been set up in the prow and, as the boat ploughed south through the aquamarine waters, its melodies coaxed people on to their feet. Soon the top deck was alive with gyrating bodies.

'I have a confession to make,' Shafe said, relaxing in the less frantic pace down below. 'When these six weeks started, I wasn't too sure how they'd work out. I don't mean from the angle of us getting together—though there were problems enough there—but you, me and Emma living together for forty-five consecutive days. As you pointed out, spending so long in each other's company was a totally new experience.'

'You were frightened family life would turn out to be humdrum?' Keri grinned.

He gave a sheepish smile. 'Something like that did occur to me.'

'And to me. And?'

'And the longer the three of us are together, the more I like it. I guess it'd be accurate to say I've become addicted.' In the prow, the steel band brought one tune to an end and promptly started into another. 'Shall we dance? Baz'll look after Emma, and as I remember it you pack a very mean hip swing.'

Keri took hold of his hand. 'Let's.'

But their daughter had different ideas.

'"Ring Roses",' she demanded as they got to their feet.

'Here? Now?' Shafe asked. 'You wouldn't settle for "Ride a Cock Horse" instead?'

'"Ring Roses",' repeated Emma.

He looked at Keri. 'I'm game if you are. Though I should stress that the only reason I'm prepared to make a fool of myself in public is because I'm madly in love with the pair of you.'

'Ditto,' she declared, kissing him.

'Di—itto,' copied Emma.

So while everyone on the top deck boogied frantically, three people who loved each other played 'Ring-o-Roses' down below.

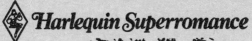

Harlequin Superromance

**Here are the longer, more involving stories you
have been waiting for... Superromance.**

Modern, believable novels of love, full of the complex
joys and heartaches of real people.

Intriguing conflicts based on today's constantly
changing life-styles.

Four new titles every month.
Available wherever paperbacks are sold.

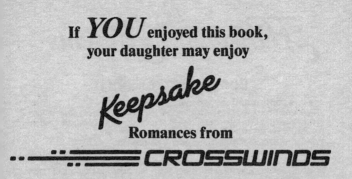

Harlequin Presents

Coming Next Month

Available in January wherever paperback books are sold, or through
Harlequin Reader Service:

In the U.S.
901 Fuhrmann Blvd.
P.O. Box 1397
Buffalo, N.Y. 14240-1397

In Canada
P.O. Box 603
Fort Erie, Ontario
L2A 5X3

Harlequin Historicals

Step into a world of pulsing adventure, gripping emotion and lush sensuality with these evocative love stories penned by today's best-selling authors in the highest romantic tradition. Pursuing their passionate dreams against a backdrop of the past's most colorful and dramatic moments, our vibrant heroines and dashing heroes will make history come alive for you.

Watch for two new Harlequin Historicals each month, available wherever Harlequin books are sold. History was never so much fun—you won't want to miss a single moment!

GHIST-1